THE VILLAGE CRICKET TOUR

By the same author

THE VILLAGE CRICKET TOUR

Vernon Coleman

Chilton Designs

Chilton Designs Publishers
Preston House, Kentisbury, Barnstaple, Devon EX31 4NH

This book is copyright. No part may be reproduced by any process without written permission. Inquiries should be addressed to the publishers.

First published in the United Kingdom by Chilton Designs in 1990.

Copyright © Vernon Coleman 1990

Set by Bath Press Integraphics, Avon
Printed by The Bath Press, Avon

British Library Cataloguing in Publication Data
Coleman, Vernon, *1946–*
    The village cricket tour.
    I. Title
    823.914[F]

    ISBN 0–9503527–3–X

DEDICATION

To Russell Smith, a cricketer and a gentleman

THE VILLAGE CRICKET TOUR

Vernon Coleman

The Touring Party (in order of appearance)

1. The author – middle order batsman and medium pace bowler. More adept with the pen than with either bat or ball.
2. Oily – charming but unpredictable. Middle order batsman and enthusiastic medium pace bowler with a penchant for fast cars and fast women.
3. Arthur – wicket keeper whose other hobby is drinking.
4. Simon – 17 year old leg spinner who has never been away from home before.
5. Wodger – our captain. Reliable school teacher who enjoys being in charge. Opening batsman and occasional bowler of indeterminate style.
6. Sergeant Tate – pompous sergeant and opening batsman.
7. June – Sergeant Tate's wife. Looks like a doll but can look after herself.
8. Norman – cautious, indecisive, inoffensive accountant who bats high in the order since he is our club treasurer.
9. Jerry – aggressive builder who usually bats at number three and bowls predictable fast medium bouncers.
10. Kurt – clergyman and fast bowler.
11. Brian – insurance salesman and slow bowler who doesn't spin the ball but doesn't bowl fast enough to be classified as a medium pace bowler.
12. Sharon – buxom barmaid who wears spike heels, short skirts and tight jumpers.

CHAPTER ONE

I needed just one run for my century and we needed another five runs to beat the Australians.

Everyone said it had been a thrilling Test Match to watch but it had been an exhausting match to play in. For five days Lords had been as crowded as I've ever seen it and the outcome of the match had never been certain. At the end of the first day the advantage had been with the Australians – now it looked as though we could win.

I'd been batting for four hours and I'd had to work hard for every run I'd scored. The Australian bowlers hadn't given away anything; they'd kept the ball well pitched up and on line.

Around the ground the tension was building up. Every spectator knew that the fate of the match now rested on my shoulders. The batsman at the other end was our number eleven. He'd been playing for England for two seasons and still hadn't scored a run. It was, to be honest, the sort of situation I loved. I felt surprisingly calm and cool.

The much feared Australian fast bowler began his run up. I stayed perfectly still and the crowd quietened as he approached the wicket. I had only a fraction of a second to decide on a shot but knew automatically what I was going to do. I took two paces down the wicket and swung my bat. The ball shot straight back in the direction from which it had come; over the bowler's head and high over the boundary. It landed on the pavilion balcony.

I stood for a second, happy and exhausted, and then felt someone urgently prodding my arm to attract my attention.

1

'Wake up!' cried Oily.

Reluctantly, I did as I was ordered. Slowly I returned to reality.

'Where am I?' I asked, sleepily. I looked across to my right at the driver of the car, the man who had woken me by punching my arm. I tried to rub the soreness away.

Everything seemed to happen in slow motion, like a film played at one tenth its normal speed. Oily's arms were straight and he was grimacing. He was leaning back so that he could put more pressure on the brake pedal.

I turned my head frontwards again just in time to see our bonnet crumple as it smashed noisily into the back of a slow moving lorry. A lot of things happened all at once. I could hear the glass in the headlights breaking and I could see steam escaping from the radiator. I could see the bonnet crumple upwards, as though it was made of silver foil, and I felt my seat belt tighten as my body thrust forwards against it. I felt a pain in my left knee as it crashed into the padded fascia at the front of the car.

'I wanted you to see this happen!' shouted Oily. 'I might need you as a witness.'

The accident had no effect at all on the speed of the lorry in front of us but we slowed down dramatically. For a hundred yards or so the remains of our bonnet remained firmly attached to its tailgate and then, slowly a gap appeared as the lorry gradually pulled away from us.

'Did you see that moron?' asked Oily, shaking his head in disbelief. His hands were gripping the steering wheel so tightly that his knuckles were white.

'What moron?'

'In the middle lane,' Oily replied. 'I tried to pull out to overtake but he kept me boxed in!'

A great cloud of steam escaped from the bonnet and completely obliterated our view of the road ahead. I heard a tinny but expensive sound as a piece of metal fell from the front of the car and then felt two distinct bumps as we drove over it. Almost immediately afterwards the car swerved to the left as the front nearside tyre punctured.

'What were you doing in the inside lane?' I asked him. 'You drive too fast to be in the inside lane.'

'Its safer,' said Oily without embarrassment. 'The police always watch the outside lane. I just hop round the lorries.'

The car slowed and the cloud of steam in front of us gradually cleared. We bumped, squeaked and lurched to a halt on the hard shoulder.

It wasn't a good start.

We were on the first day of a two week cricket tour of the West Country. Our club captain, Roger Holcroft (known to everyone as 'Wodger' for reasons which become apparent the moment he opens his mouth and exhibits his total inability to roll an 'r') had arranged nine matches for our team, The Midland Parks Peripatetics (so named because we had no ground of our own but had to play our matches wherever we could find an away fixture).

For a while we'd toyed with the idea of hiring a coach. But when we'd found out how much it was going to cost we'd abandoned the idea and decided instead to travel in three cars; Sergeant Tate's seven year old Vauxhall, Jerry Dixon's eleven year old Volvo estate and Oily Wragge's virtually brand new Jaguar.

You might have thought that there would have been keen competition to travel in Oily Wragge's Jaguar with its eight speaker stereo system, full climate control air conditioning and leather upholstery. But you'd have been wrong. Everyone admired the car but no one wanted to travel in it if he was driving. Oily's attitude towards motor cars has always been distinctly Gallic. Bumps and dents don't worry him at all. His contempt for the highway code is matched only by his Toad like disrespect for the police and other road-users.

I'd known Oily Wragge for many years. We'd gone to school together, discovered alcohol, girls and pain together and were now drifting inexorably into middle age together. Once tall and elegant but now developing just the slightest hint of a paunch Oily was described by his friends as gregarious, jolly, charming and outgoing. Those who disliked him complained that he was noisy, unpredictable and unreliable. The truth was that he was all these things.

In his late teens Oily had served a brief and unstructured apprenticeship in his father's meat packing factory. All my relatives insisted that Oily would pay for his indolence and assured me that I would discover that hard work would earn me far greater rewards. This, of course, was nonsense. By the time he was thirty Oily had inherited a large and profitable business about which he knew next to nothing. In a hard week he worked five or six hours, if sitting in an office signing papers can be described as work. The business was run for him by a team of efficient and grossly underpaid managers who had been trained and installed by his father.

Stories about Oily abound but I can probably best describe his character by describing the way he beats traffic queues.

When he finds himself becoming part of a slow moving or stationary row of traffic Oily always follows the same well rehearsed and invariably effective procedure. He turns on his headlights, puts a finger on his horn and drives straight down the middle of the road. Then, when he gets to the cause of the obstruction, he leaps out of his car and rushes up to anyone who seems to be in charge.

'Do you need a doctor?' he cries; cool, sharp urgency colouring his voice.

If the hold up has been caused by a set of faulty traffic lights, a team of road menders or an unusually heavy flow of traffic Oily will smile with relief and get back into his car. Workmen always consider him public spirited and other motorists always obediently and respectfully let him in at the head of the queue. Since his car is by now blocking the road they have little choice.

If, on the other hand, the hold up has been caused by an accident and those in attendance claim that they do indeed need the services of a doctor Oily will leap back into his car, shout: 'I'll get one!' and use his car telephone to ring for whatever public services seem appropriate.

When Oily first mastered this ploy car telephones were a rarity and his presence at genuine accidents was greeted with enthusiasm. Recently, however, he complained to me that in some parts of England it can be difficult to get within a mile of an accident because every available space will be taken up with motorists using their car telephones to ring for help.

On this occasion, Oily's car telephone proved to be a boon. While whisps of steam still spiralled up from the front of the car he called the RAC and asked for assistance.

4

I twisted round so that I could look into the back of the car while he gave the emergency services operator details of where we could be found.

There were two passengers in the back: Arthur Young, our 56 year old wicket keeper, and Simon Lloyd, a 15 year old leg spinner who'd never been away from home before and whose mother had spent fifteen minutes making me swear to ensure that no harm befell him and that he returned to her bosom as innocent of vice as he had left it.

Arthur had a broad smile on his face but was unconscious. An empty hip flask lay on his lap and explained both the smile and the lack of interest in our predicament.

Simon was white and still looked terrified. He had never travelled with Oily before and this was almost certainly his first road traffic accident. I smiled and winked at him in the slight hope that this would reassure him but my optimism was unfounded. He opened his mouth to say something and then shut it again without a word escaping.

'Its nothing to worry about,' I whispered. Oily was giving his telephone number.

Simon opened his mouth again. This time a croaking sound escaped.

'Did you get that bastard's number?' Oily asked me.

I turned my head and looked at him. For a moment I didn't know what he meant.

'That bastard in the red Ford,' explained Oily. 'The one who boxed me in.'

'Sorry!' I said.

Oily shrugged, said goodbye to the operator and put the telephone down.

'You all right, kid?' he asked, twisting his rear view mirror so that he could check on Simon. He didn't bother to look at Arthur.

Simon opened his mouth for the third time and was violently sick.

* * *

'These cricket tours can be pretty fraught with danger,' said Oily. 'You never know what's going to happen.'

5

We were sitting on the motorway embankment watching the traffic stream past. Both nearside doors of the car were open in an attempt to dilute the acrid smell of Simon's second hand lunch. The front of the Jaguar looked distinctly unhappy; the headlights, the radiator, the bumper, the bonnet and both front wings all looked to be beyond repair; the nearside front tyre was flat. Arthur Young was the only occupant of the car. He still hadn't woken up and still had the same innocent smile on his face. Simon was sitting on the embankment a couple of yards away, his head buried in his hands. He was wearing his cricket shirt and trousers – the first clothes that had come to hand when Oily had opened his suitcase. His luncheon soiled clothes had been rolled into a bundle, wrapped in a plastic bag and stuffed into the boot.

'I once had a friend who used to captain a cricket team called The Marauders,' Oily went on. 'All the members of the team drank at the same public house in the middle of Bolton. One summer they decided that they'd go away together on a cricket tour.'

'There was,' said Oily, 'a considerable amount of discussion about just where they should go. After several hours the team was divided into two equal groups. Half of them wanted to go to Corfu and play cricket under the Mediterranean sun. The other half wanted to go to Canada. The members who favoured Corfu argued that the weather in the Mediterranean would be reliable and bright and would make a pleasant change for cricketers brought up on damp pitches, chilly winds and soggy outfields. The group supporting a Canadian tour were being staunchly and unpredictably patriotic. They said the Canadians would appreciate a tour from the Mother Country.'

'So where did they go?' I asked.

'Cornwall,' replied Oily. 'The club was split in two and the captain had the casting vote.'

'Fair enough,' I nodded. Cricket club captains are, as a breed, strong minded and accustomed to using their power.

'I don't know whether it was the fact that they were going to Cornwall or the natural effect of time,' Oily went on, 'but by the time the tour started there were only five people left who were interested in it. Six if you count the captain.'

'As a side it wasn't all that well balanced,' said Oily. 'They had three specialist opening batsmen and three leg spinners.'

'The first match was in Truro on a lovely little ground where the captain's uncle was President. The touring party was supplemented with a fast bowling farm labourer, a wicket keeping tractor driver and two ice cream salesmen, both of whom were enthusiastic leg spinners.'

'Lots of strength and depth in the leg spinning department,' I commented.

'Absolutely,' agreed Oily. 'They completed the team by press ganging a ten year old boy who'd gone out looking for mushrooms.'

'Not surprisingly the visitors lost the match by a fistful of runs but everyone had such a good time that when they left Truro the wicket keeping tractor driver and the two ice cream salesmen went with them – all travelling in the ice cream van.'

'The next match was in Padstow,' Oily continued. 'There the team was supplemented by a taxi driver who'd had a row with his wife and a keen club cricketer from Dartford who was on holiday with his family. The club cricketer was a medium pace bowler and a middle order batsman and the taxi driver was a leg spinner.'

'How much did they lose by?' I asked.

'Can't remember,' replied Oily. 'Quite a lot.' He paused and watched an RAC service van drive straight past us at about sixty miles an hour. By the time we were on our feet, waving our arms in an attempt to attract the driver's attention, he was almost out of sight.

'When they left Padstow,' he said, settling back down on the embankment, 'the taxi driver and the man from Dartford went with them. The man from Dartford had his wife and four miserable children with him. Their next match was in Penzance and a rough spot on the pitch enabled the leg spinners to take a lot of wickets very cheaply. It was apparently such a good match that when The Marauders left for Liskeard four members of the home team left with them. That meant that when they arrived they had four players to spare and were able to lend the home team two leg spinners, an opening bat and an umpire.'

'After that things got slowly out of hand,' said Oily. 'By the time they arrived in Redruth they'd become a convoy and they had enough players to field a first and a second eleven.'

'As far as I know they're all still down there in Redruth,' concluded Oily.

'Eight of the tourists married local girls and even the man from Dartford settled down there. The captain's wife did get a letter at Christmas inviting her to go down and join the team but no one else heard anything from them.'

Oily lay back on the grass and folded his arms across his chest. I was the only one to see the RAC breakdown van speed back up on the other side of the motorway. He slowed a little as he went by and I saw the driver gesticulating to show that he would turn round and be back with us as soon as he could.

Since there seemed little else to do I too lay back on the grass. I closed my eyes and wondered, not for the first time, whether I'd done the right thing in deciding to join the tour.

To be perfectly honest I had never really intended to go on the tour at all.

When the captain had asked about my availability I'd been honoured, of course, but I hadn't taken the invitation too seriously.

When I'd got home that evening I'd mentioned the invitation almost in passing.

'I shan't go, of course,' I said. 'I wouldn't dream of leaving you for a fortnight.'

I'd been disappointed in my wife's attitude.

'Of course you must go!' she insisted, without a moment's hesitation.

Her response came as quite a surprise. I'd been relying on her to provide me with an excellent excuse for not going. If I'm perfectly honest I had, I suppose, envisaged using the tour to gain a considerable number of brownie points all round. I'd rather seen myself as something of a martyr; selflessly abandoning my place on the tour so that I could stay at home and be with her and the children.

'Sorry chaps,' I'd heard myself saying. 'Really miffed at not being able to join you and all that but I can't possibly leave the little woman for that long. She went quite hysterical when I mentioned the idea. Said she wouldn't be able to cope and threatened to throw herself off the roof if I didn't promise on the spot to stay at home.'

That's what I'd imagined myself saying but it didn't go like that at all.

'The exercise will do you good,' she told me.

'It would have been fun,' I murmured. 'But its much too long to be away from home.'

'Nonsense,' she said. 'I'll take the children away to the seaside. It'll give us a great chance to get in some serious sunbathing.'

'What if there's an emergency?' I heard myself asking.

But I'd been talking to myself. Overcome with grief my wife had rushed off to telephone our travel agent and ask him to send some holiday brochures round.

'Somewhere sunny – Spain, Italy or the South of France,' I heard her say.

As I lay back on the grassy motorway embankment I could almost imagine that I was with them; soaking up the sun on some Mediterranean beach. Only the sound and smell of the endless streams of roaring traffic spoilt the illusion.

Five minutes later the RAC van drew up beside Oily's Jaguar.

* * *

To my surprise the damage wasn't quite as terminal as it had at first appeared.

The RAC man towed us to the nearest Jaguar garage. There, after Oily had filled his grubby hands with crisp bank notes the chief mechanic agreed to push our car to the front of the queue. While Arthur continued to sleep in the back of the car Oily, Simon and I sought temporary refuge in a nearby cafe, where we ordered three bacon sandwiches and three large mugs of tea.

As we munched and slurped out way through our artery clogging feast I couldn't help wondering how the rest of the team was getting on.

* * *

CHAPTER TWO

We'd met at 9 o'clock that morning outside the main gates of the Walsall Arboretum.

Our team captain, Wodger Holcroft had been waiting outside the Arboretum when I'd arrived with Oily. Efficient and capable as ever Wodger had ticked off our names on the clip board he was carrying. Wodger is a school-teacher through and through and is never happier than when ticking names off from a long list. Wodger is so reliable that people around him tend to become incompetent, incapable and totally dependent upon him within minutes of meeting him. He so clearly enjoys being in charge that most people simply allow him to take over and organise their lives for them.

Wodger is one of our opening batsmen. The other is Sergeant Tate. I don't know his first name and I'm not sure that he has one. Even if he has I doubt if anyone has ever used it. It would be cruel to describe him as pompous or standoffish but I've even heard his mother address him as 'Sergeant'. Sergeant Tate has been a member of our local constabulary for two decades and regards crime as a personal affront.

Sergeant Tate looks as though he was constructed rather hastily by a building firm that was overly conscious of its potential liability to late completion penalties. A noticeable hormonal imbalance gave him a prominent forehead, protruding jaw and massive hands. Years of activity in the police gymnasium have given him acres of bulging muscle.

When Oily and I arrived Sergeant Tate was deep in conversation with his wife, June.

June is as tiny as her husband is huge. She is, I guess, just about five feet tall. She looks a little bit like a doll and dresses like one too. In her case, however, appearances are extremely deceptive. She may look fragile but she can look after herself. Like everyone else she refers to her fiercesome husband as 'Sergeant' but unlike everyone else she never listens to anything he says. She bullies him mercilessly.

Norman Wilkes and Jerry Dixon are our other two senior batsmen.

Norman is an accountant and it isn't difficult to guess his profession. He is one of those people who was clearly destined to be an accountant from childhood. Still only in his mid thirties he is tubby, bespectacled and balding. He looks much older than he is.

Desperately inoffensive and always careful to avoid doing anything that could be considered contentious or risky Norman does not look like a great batsman. In his case appearances are not deceptive. He is, however, our club treasurer and the only member of the team who can do our accounts and is, therefore, guaranteed a prime batting spot. People who don't know Norman very well sometimes claim that he is rather overly cautious and often pedantic. Those of us who know him well know that in addition to these qualities Norman is also dull and rather humourless.

Norman is famous among those who know him for being exceptionally careful before making decisions. I remember once sharing a hotel room with him when we went down to Lords together to watch a couple of days of Test Match cricket. It was an exquisitely painful experience.

Norman had taken two suitcases full of clothes with him although we were only due to be away from home for one night. As soon as we arrived in our room Norman insisted on unpacking and hanging up his shirts, trousers and jackets. He chose two drawers in the dressing table and allocated the other two to me although I assured him that he could have all four. I tried to explain how silly I'd feel keeping each of my socks in a separate drawer.

Watching Norman dress in the morning was quite an experience. First of all he put on a pair of socks. Then he pulled on some underpants and added a shirt. Then he wandered around the room trying to decide which suit to put on. When he'd decided on a suit he discovered that the socks weren't quite right for it and so he took them off, rolled them up carefully and exchanged them for a more appropriate pair.

Next, he decided that the shirt wasn't quite perfect either. So that had to come off and go back into the wardrobe. Having changed his shirt he looked for a tie and discovered that he had forgotten to pack the only tie that could possibly go with that shirt. And so off came the suit trousers, the shirt and the socks. Then he went back to the original socks and another suit.

When we finally got down into the dining room things were just as bad there. For the life of him Norman just couldn't make decisions. Choosing between tea and coffee and toast and croissants was bad enough but when the waitress came to ask him whether he wanted eggs and bacon; eggs and sausage and bacon; eggs and sausage; sausage and bacon; eggs, bacon and tomato; eggs, bacon, tomato and fried bread or eggs on toast he simply froze and became quite incapable of offering her any sort of instruction.

After breakfast Norman spent twenty minutes trying to decide what newspaper to buy, whether or not to clean his teeth and whether or not to change his suit again. It turned out that the suit he was already wearing had only been for breakfast.

I don't think Norman enjoys being so indecisive. It's just something he inherited. I once asked him how he'd ever managed to get married or decide on a career. He told me that he met his wife when he was six years old and that she'd asked him to marry her when he'd lent her his ruler. He said it was his wife who decided on a suitable career.

Jerry Dixon is a completely different character. He works as a builder and has enough aggression for at least two people. I sometimes think that he probably has Norman's share. Not long ago he had to appear in the local magistrates court after threatening to ram a drainpipe down a customers throat. He astounded the court when, after being asked a question by the magistrate, he informed the gentleman on the bench that he would be obliged if he would speak up a little.

On another occasion a man in a public house cracked what

he thought was a joke about 'Jerry builders'. Jerry was not amused by this and it took two of us nearly half an hour to persuade him that impaling the humourist on an upturned chair leg would cause more problems than it would solve. Jerry usually bats at number three for us and clubs against whom we play regularly claim that his presence in our team makes finding umpires particularly difficult. I think this is probably unfair for it's a long time since the incident with the stump and the heavy roller.

Our strike bowler is a local clergyman called Kurt Meitner. Everyone assumes he is German because of his name but he's as English as the next man who in our team happens to be Brian O'Toole. Brian is a slow bowler. He doesn't spin the ball at all but he doesn't bowl fast enough to be a fast bowler or even a medium pace bowler.

Our other regular player is Hermann Potter. Hermann is a medium pace bowler and middle order batsman (which means, of course, that he can't bowl very well and doesn't bat too well either). Hermann wanted to come on the tour but his wife wouldn't let him. She said she wanted the kitchen decorating.

Young Simon, a schoolboy prodigy who bowls leg spinners and Arthur Young, our wicket keeper, were told by Wodger that they would be travelling with Oily and I. Wodger didn't really want to send Simon with us but Simon's mother had, for reasons best known to herself, decided that I would be a good influence on him. It didn't really matter who Arthur travelled with since he is rarely aware of his surroundings.

Wodger announced that Sergeant Tate, Norman and the vicar would be travelling with him while Brian would travel with Jerry in his old Volvo. Wodger does not have much faith in Jerry's Volvo and I suspect that he wanted to minimise the chances of losing more than two of his players at once.

As we were about to climb into our cars and set off for our first match on the North Devon coast Wodger announced that we would not be driving in formation but would be free to make our own way to the first venue.

This was a sensible decision since Oily is incapable of driving as slowly as the sort of speed that Wodger regards as reckless.

Wodger's favourite speed is somewhere between 25 and 30

miles per hour and although Oily must pass through this land-mark at least twice on each journey it is not a speed he favours. Oily claims that Wodger only ever uses two forward gears. One Saturday last season Oily challenged Wodger to a race between the Pigeons Breast public house in Aldridge and the main gates of the Walsall Arboretum. Oily, handicapping him-self by confining himself to reverse gear, still managed to win by nearly a mile.

Oily had started to pull away from the kerb when I noticed that Sergeant Tate was still standing on the pavement with his wife. They were clearly involved in what is, I believe, officially known as a domestic dispute. I told Oily to stop for a moment.

We watched in amazement as Sergeant Tate stepped across to Wodger's car, bent down and held the door open while the vicar got out. The vicar spoke to Sergeant Tate, smiled, nodded and then walked over to Jerry's Volvo. Then, with Sergeant Tate still holding the car door open June Tate got in!

I got out and went over to Wodger's car to see what was happening.

'June is coming with us,' said Wodger, speaking through clenched teeth.

I looked into the back of the car where June was sitting alongside Norman the accountant.

June just looked straight ahead as though she hadn't seen me.

Wodger turned to Sergeant Tate as though expecting help but none came.

'June says that if Sergeant Tate is going to the West Country for two weeks then she's going as well,' said Wodger.

I looked across at the police sergeant in disbelief and then looked back at Wodger. 'But its a cricket tour!' I said. 'Wives don't go on cricket tours.'

But June clearly was not about to allow protocol to stand in her way.

I walked back to Oily's car, got in and told him the news.

Four hours later we were sitting in a transport cafe some-where in Somerset while the front end of the Jaguar was rebuilt.

14

Inspired by Oily's banknotes the mechanic managed to finish the running repairs to the Jaguar in a couple of hours. The headlamps still didn't work and the bonnet had to be held shut with the aid of a length of wire but the car was driveable. The punctured tyre had been replaced, the loose bodywork removed and the radiator repaired.

In our absence Arthur had woken but finding himself alone had simply continued with his favourite hobby. Few things shake or startle Arthur and as a regular passenger in cars driven by Oily he is now accustomed to the sounds of bodywork being pulled and hammered back into shape. When we arrived he was sitting up in the back of the car sipping at his beloved hip flask. However long a journey may be Arthur's hip flask never stays empty for long. How it gets refilled I have no idea.

Arthur is in his mid fifties. He retired from his position as a local government officer some time ago and is an enthusiastic cricket player and supporter. As a young man he once had a trial for Worcestershire but, sadly, never actually played first class cricket. These days, despite his pickled liver and constant state of inebriation he is still one of the best wicket keepers I've ever played with.

Unlike younger, more athletic players Arthur never throws himself around. I don't think he's ever had a grass stain on his trousers or shirt since I've known him. He never makes a fuss and to opposition batsmen simply seems to have a happy knack of being in the right place at the right time (or, as far as they are concerned, the wrong place at the wrong time). He is unfailingly courteous and always apologies to the batsmen he dismisses.

Arthur's marriage broke down about five years ago when his wife ran off with a local income tax inspector. The impact of this domestic disruption can be judged from the fact that it was ten days before Arthur noticed that his wife was missing and another week after that before his half hearted investigations proved that she had gone for good. She had moved to a house three doors away where she still lives. Arthur's current domestic arrangements would probably be regarded by some as slightly bizarre for he now pays his wife to do his laundry, shopping and cleaning. They never bothered to get divorced.

After Oily had given the mechanic more money the four of us continued on our journey to North Devon. Our first match had been fixed against the village team at Queen's Lapford – a tiny village just outside the twin coastal resorts of Lynton and Lynmouth – and on the advice of the local cricket club secretary Wodger had booked us all accommodation at a public house called the Duck and Puddle.

*   *   *

CHAPTER THREE

Despite our delay we arrived at the Duck and Puddle ahead of the rest of the team. Wodger, as I have already explained, is a slow driver. Jerry would like to drive faster but his ancient Volvo is slow to respond and few journeys on British motorways are long enough to enable it to reach its top speed of 55 miles per hour. We signed in, put our bags in our rooms and settled down in the public bar.

During the last few years most country pubs have been taken over by large breweries. However successful a small country pub may have been while run independently the breweries always want to change things. A small pub that is warmed with a log fire and offers its patrons home cured ham will be gutted. The log fire will be replaced with central heating and the thick slices of home cured ham will be replaced with thin slices of plastic meat served with French Fries rather than chips. The old red leather chairs and stools and genuine brass topped tables will be replaced with banquettes covered in purple velvet and chipboard tables fitted with built in video games. The dart board will be banished and the jar of pickled eggs replaced with stuffed olives.

Fortunately, the Duck and Puddle had escaped this heavy handed treatment and, for the time being at least, remained in private hands. The landlord liked his pub so much that instead of standing behind the bar and serving the customers he sat as close as possible to his raging log fire. Outside the remains of the day's sunshine was still warm enough for a few customers to be sitting sipping their beer at trestle tables. But the landlord clearly liked a log fire and wasn't the sort of man to allow trivial and unpredictable forces like the weather to interfere with life.

Behind the bar drinks and food were served by a pair of cheerful barmaids – one blonde and one brunette. It is traditional to describe barmaids as buxom but calling the two barmaids at the Duck and Puddle buxom would be rather like calling Lords a cricket ground. The description is accurate but it doesn't do the subject justice. The blonde was the older of the two, in her early forties I suppose, and she had a wit as sharp as cheesewire. The brunette seemed to be in her mid twenties and appeared, by comparison, rather modest. They were both good looking rather than merely pretty and seemed to be competing in their efforts to display their physical charms to best effect.

While Arthur sipped at a large whisky and Simon wrote a lengthy letter home to his mother Oily and I sat on stools at the bar and admired the views on the other side of the counter.

'Do you think young Simon is all right?' Oily asked me, nodding his head slightly in the direction of our young prodigy.

'He's fine,' I assured him.

'He's very quiet.'

'He's fifteen.'

'His mother seems a bit possessive,' said Oily, stuffing a handful of peanuts into his mouth.

'His father left home when he was a kid,' I explained, 'and he's an only child.'

'Oh God!' said Oily, pouring beer after the peanuts. 'No girlfriends, I don't suppose?'

'Not that I know of.'

Noticing that our glasses were nearly empty the brunette barmaid came towards us. She asked us if we wanted refills by raising an eyebrow.

Oily smiled at her and she smiled back. I toyed with the idea of reminding him of what had happened at Swansea earlier in the season but decided not to bother. Things like that just don't happen twice.

It was another hour before Jerry, the vicar and Brian arrived and half an hour after that before Wodger turned up with Norman and Sergeant and Mrs Tate. By then Simon had gone to bed, Arthur had drifted into unconsciousness again and Oily and I had eaten all of the peanuts and most of the pickled eggs. We all shook hands, greeting one another as though we had been parted for at least a decade, and congratulated one another on our navigational skills and resourcefulness in successfully finding the Duck and Puddle. Then we all went to bed.

*   *   *

The match was due to begin at the Queens Lapford cricket ground at 2.00 pm and at breakfast the following morning there was a general air of excitement hovering over the bacon and eggs.

Inevitably, our captain was unable to share our pleasure. He had many responsibilities weighing him down. Arthur, our wicket keeper, was still unconscious upstairs. Simon was homesick and kept bursting into tears. Sergeant Tate and his wife weren't speaking to one another or, indeed, to anyone else. And Oily seemed to have disappeared.

In addition Wodger had to find an eleventh man.

At half past eight that morning Wodger had telephoned the secretary of the Queens Lapford cricket club to ask if he could spare a player. But the request had fallen on stony ground. The Queens Lapford secretary explained that he'd had difficulty enough finding eleven fit players and two umpires. There was, he assured Wodger, absolutely no chance of discovering any 'spare' cricketers by 2.00 pm that afternoon.

By twelve thirty the situation had improved only to the extent that Oily had reappeared. He looked exhausted but his presence cheered Wodger slightly as he sat hunched over his Filofax still trying to create an eleven man team out of ten players.

'What about June?' asked Oily, dipping a slice of herbal sausage into the centre of his egg. Officially breakfast had finished at 10.00 am and only cold lunches were being served but Oily didn't seem to have had any difficulty in obtaining a full cooked breakfast.

Wodger looked puzzled. 'June?' He thought for a moment and then shook his head. 'We didn't have any pwoblems with

19

players in June.'

'Not that June!,' said Oily, stuffing a whole mushroom into his mouth.

Wodger and the rest of us had to wait for the best part of a minute for Oily to finish his mushroom and explain what he meant.

'June Tate!' he said at last.

'June Tate? What about her?'

'We need an eleventh player,' pointed out Oily. 'Why not see if she can play?'

'June?' said Wodger, incredulously. 'But ...,' he paused and stuttered, 'she's a ...' he seemed to find the whole idea incomprehensibly stupid, 'she's a ... *woman!*'

'Thank God you noticed,' said Oily, piercing a sliver of bacon and then adding a square of fried bread to his fork.

'There doesn't seem to be any real alternative,' I said. 'Apart from playing a man short.'

'But she's a woman!' was all that Wodger could say.

Eventually even Wodger the misogynist realised that Oily's suggestion made a certain amount of sense. He left the table and set off in search of our eleventh player.

* * *

It would, I think, be reasonable to describe the atmosphere in the visitors dressing room at the Queens Lapford cricket club as 'strained.'

The Queens Lapford captain had been slightly surprised when Wodger told him that we would be fielding a female but he didn't object. The objection came instead from Sergeant Tate.

I've never seen a man go purple before. I've *heard* of people going purple. And I've seen people go a bit purplish. But every bit of Sergeant Tate that was visible went bright purple and stayed that colour. He looked dangerously apoplectic and an entirely unsuitable candidate for life insurance.

He took it badly when Wodger told him that there would be two 'Tates' on the scorecard. But when his wife appeared in the dressing room and proceeded to dress herself in one of Norman's spare shirts and a pair of the vicar's shorts Sergeant Tate looked so discomfited that it was no longer quite so easy to hide one's amusement. I thought that Oily's generous offer to lend June his spare 'box' was poorly timed.

June Tate seemed to enjoy it all. She ignored her churlish and bad tempered husband and giggled girlishly when the vicar's shorts proved too big for her and fell down around her ankles.

'Where would you like to field?' asked Wodger as I looked out of the pavilion window while June struggled to protect her modesty with one of Norman's ties. (Norman is the only man I know who always has a complete change of clothes available – including a spare tie). She was using the tie to hold up the vicar's rather baggy shorts.

Wodger always asks me this before a match. And he always pretends that it is a question worth answering. It isn't, of course. When he first started asking me this I always thought carefully before answering. I would look around the ground and choose a spot where I wouldn't have too much sun in my eyes, where I could rely on a little shade when the sun was at its highest and where I would be unlikely to see too much of the action.

'Just over there would do very nicely,' I would say. 'Close to that girl in the blue dress.'

And Wodger would shake his head sadly and tell me that the spot I'd picked was already spoken for.

Wherever I chose would already be earmarked for some other player.

So these days I regard the question as a rhetorical one, a courtesy from a captain who would like to be old fashioned.

'Anywhere you like, captain,' I replied. 'I'm in your hands.'

At five to two Wodger lost the toss (he always does), and was told that we would be fielding, and so at two pm precisely we trooped out onto the field for the first match of our tour.

The Queens Lapford cricket ground is one of the most beautiful I've ever seen. Unlike many village cricket fields it is remarkably flat and well maintained. There is, however, one peculiarity about the Queens Lapford ground. On its northern side it is bordered not by a pleasant hedge or a screen of trees but by a four hundred foot sheer drop down into the Bristol Channel.

From the pavilion this feature is not immediately obvious.

21

It is true that on the far side of the pitch all one can see is sky but I had innocently assumed that this merely reflected the fact that the ground was rather high up. I had erroneously assumed that the land on the far side of the pitch sloped gently downwards.

It was Brian O'Toole who first discovered the truth about this remarkable local feature. Standing gingerly about two feet away from the edge he called the rest of us over to him.

'I nearly fell over there!' he complained, pointing unnecessarily at the cliff edge. A pair of seagulls, disturbed by our presence, suddenly flew up from the face of the cliff and sent us scurrying backwards in surprise.

'Nothing to worry about, Bwian,' said Wodger confidently. He looked around in vain for some sign showing where the boundary was. 'I'd better go and ask someone what the local wules are,' he added, before hobbling off in the direction of the pavilion. Wodger suffers with his feet and is something of a martyr to them.

'I'm not fielding anywhere near here,' said Brian to no one in particular. Brian sells insurance for a living and his professional knowledge and skills enable him to combine pessimism and hypochondriasis with an unusual level of scientific efficiency. He stepped back another pace and took a small, well thumbed limp covered book from his back pocket.

We waited, knowing what was coming and yet nonetheless curious.

'Twenty two people fell from cliff tops last year,' he announced somberly, reading from his pocket volume.

We all edged backwards a little, away from the cliff edge, anxious lest a breeze should suddenly appear and whisk one of us to our death. Jerry Dixon stamped timidly on the turf, his stamping foot stretched out as far as it would reach. He seemed to be testing the cliff edge to see how solid it was.

Brian took out a large, white, linen handkerchief and blew his nose boisterously. He stuffed his insurance man's pocket guide back into his back trouser pocket.

'The cliff edge is the boundawy,' cried Wodger, hobbling back in our direction. He seemed cheerful. 'Their captain says would we please do our best to stop the ball going over the edge because they can only get balls back at low tide from a boat.'

We looked at him but no one said anything.

'Wather quaint, don't you think?' He grinned at each of us in turn but no one grinned back at him.

'You can field here,' said Jerry.

'Ah, well, I'm at slip, as usual . . .' Wodger looked around. No one spoke a word. 'But, er, if thats, er, yes, of course, I'll field here.'

Tentatively, he stepped across towards the cliff edge. He peered over and paled when he saw the extent of the drop.

Noticing that the two umpires and the two batsmen had already emerged from the pavilion and were standing in the middle of the pitch waiting for us Wodger directed the rest of us to our positions. He threw the ball to the vicar, invariably our opening bowler and a man who does not allow the nature of his profession to interfere with his apparent intention of using the ball to drill a hole clean through the head of every batsman he faces.

The vicar's opening spell was not as successful as it has been in the past and by three o'clock the home side had still not lost a wicket. Our four best bowlers, Simon the leg spinner, Brian the slow bowler, Jerry (who bowls what he describes as medium pace in-swingers) and the vicar had suffered equally at the hands of the Queens Lapford opening pair.

The only excitement had occurred after about thirty minutes of the innings when one of the batsmen hit the ball high over Wodger's head. Wodger, running backwards and keeping his eye on the ball was about ten yards away from the cliff edge when the rest of us realised what was happening. Fortunately, Jerry, who was fielding nearby, managed to reach Wodger and bring him down with an excellent low tackle several yards short of oblivion.

By four thirty, however, things had changed dramatically. They had lost six wickets and four balls and Wodger was looking very pleased with himself. He had brought himself on in desperation but his slow left arm bowling had unexpectedly tied the opposition batsmen in knots. He'd taken four wickets for the first time in his career and Simon and Brian had a wicket each.

By five the home side innings was over. They had amassed

a total of 127 and Wodger had taken 5 for 38. It is a strange but nevertheless true fact of life that nothing gives a bowler more satisfaction than scoring a few runs and nothing gives a batsman more pleasure than taking a few unexpected wickets. At tea Wodger was glowing with pride, pleasure and bonhomie. If he'd been a cat he would have purred. The only fly contaminating his ointment was the knowledge that Sergeant Tate was still refusing to talk to anyone.

But our captain is made of stern stuff and when he and the Sergeant strode out to the wicket we were filled with confidence.

What happened next was as depressing as it was predictable.

The first ball was slightly short of a good length and just outside the off stump. Nine times out of ten Wodger would have ignored it and allowed it to go past harmlessly. But he was overflowing with confidence and could not resist the opportunity that presented itself. He slashed wildly and the ball sped away across the grass, past where cover point would have been fielding if there had been one, and off in the direction of the cliff edge.

As the fielder patrolling the extra cover boundary ran in and one of the slip fielders ran after the ball Wodger set off down the wicket as fast as he could hobble. He was half way down the wicket before he realised that Sergeant Tate hadn't even moved. The Sergeant wasn't even watching the ball. He seemed to be hypnotised by the toes of his boots.

'Wun!' screamed Wodger.

'This end!' shouted the wicket keeper.

'Other end!' shouted the bowler.

Sergeant Tate looked up, saw his captain advancing towards him at full speed and looked around as though waking up from a dream.

'No!' he shouted.

'Wun, wun!' screamed Wodger, waving his arms and bat around in a maniacal and dangerous fashion.

Too late Sergeant Tate responded. His bulk meant that his acceleration was poor and it was, from the start, a lost cause. The extra cover fielder threw the ball in fast and low. The wicket keeper collected it neatly and had the bails off with Sergeant Tate still twelve yards out of his crease.

24

Slowly and miserably Sergeant Tate dragged himself and his bat back towards the pavilion. He looked like a man who has known better days.

It was not a good beginning but first Jerry Dixon scored a rapid 30 and then Norman Wilkes added a respectable 25 and by 7.30 pm we had reached 100 for 6 wickets. When I joined Wodger at the wicket we needed 22 to win and had 3 wickets left. And then disaster struck. Wodger was out lbw playing no stroke to a straight ball, and Simon Lloyd was out the very next ball when a fast one nipped back and removed his off bail. Two balls later the vicar, Kurt Meitner, was caught behind the wicket.

Suddenly we needed 22 runs and had only one wicket left.

When the Queens Lapford team saw tiny June staggering out to the middle with a huge pair of pads strapped to her stick like legs and a massive bat tucked under her arm they were clearly not impressed. One or two of them were clearly having difficulty suppressing smiles.

Feeling a great burden of responsibility resting on my shoulders I walked down the wicket to meet her.

'Just keep your bat tight in to your pads and play everything straight back down the middle,' I told her. 'Don't worry about the runs,' I added confidently.

June brushed a couple of stray curls out of her eyes and whispered something I didn't catch. I asked her to repeat what she'd said.

'Is my lipstick all right?' she asked. 'There's no mirror in the dressing room.'

'Its fine,' I assured her, feeling beads of sweat breaking out on my forehead.

While June and I had been talking the Queens Lapford captain had been having a word with his bowler, a tall tanned fellow whose rolled up sleeves revealed a variety of tattoos.

'Guard?' asked the umpire, looking sternly down the wicket at June.

June looked puzzled.

'What guard do you want?' asked the umpire loudly.

'Oh thats kind of you to ask,' said June. 'But I'm all right, thank you.' She pointed to her legs, 'The vicar lent me his pads,' she announced.

'Play!' growled the umpire, disapprovingly.

Grinning broadly the tattooed bowler strode purposefully up to the wicket and tossed the ball underarm down in June's direction.

Keeping her eyes firmly on the ball June moved her feet a couple of feet down the wicket and whirled her bat around her as hard as she could. The crack of willow on leather could be heard all around the ground and over by the pavilion I saw Oily cheering loudly. The brunette barmaid was standing beside him dressed in the shortest skirt I'd ever seen.

The fielders watched with horror and astonishment as the ball flew over extra cover's head and disappeared over the edge of the cliff.

Six scored. That left us needing just sixteen runs.

The umpire produced another ball from his pocket and the bowler, his face black with fury, strode back to the start of his full length run. When he passed me he was travelling at top speed. The ball flew past June, past the stumps and past the wicket-keeper.

'No ball!' cried the umpire.

A moment later he signalled to the scorer to show that four no balls should be added to our score.

Once again the bowler walked back to the start of his full length run. But this time he took a little more care. The ball was short and when it reached June it was almost head height.

June stood motionless and watched the ball as it passed her by. The fielders applauded as the wicket keeper dived and caught it.

The next ball was far more accurate and was aimed more directly at June's wicket.

June played a repeat of her first shot. And again her bat connected with the ball. Again the ball flew high over the extra cover fielder, disappearing out of sight over the cliff edge.

Another six. We needed just six more.

I walked down the wicket to June and congratulated her. 'That was fantastic!' I said. 'I thought you'd never played cricket before!'

'I haven't,' she said, 'but I used to play rounders for my school.'

I turned towards the pavilion where I could see Wodger and the rest of the team crowded onto the pavilion balcony. They were shouting and waving encouragement. Only Sergeant Tate was missing.

I started to walk back up the wicket and was met by the opposition captain and the two umpires.

'We haven't got any more balls,' said one of the umpires bluntly.

'What do you mean?' I asked him.

'That was our last ball,' explained the Queens Lapford captain.

'But you must have another one somewhere . . .'

The captain looked embarrassed and shuffled his feet. 'I'm sorry . . .' he muttered. He added something about a draw.

'I wish you'd told me it was your last ball,' said June. 'I'd have hit it somewhere else.'

When we got back to the pavilion June discovered that her husband had disappeared. He had stamped out of the pavilion in a fury when his wife had hit her first ball for six.

*   *   *

CHAPTER FOUR

We stayed at the Duck and Puddle again that evening and celebrated our brush with success in the bar.

By half past ten a good deal of alcohol had been consumed and sobriety was not our strong point. Wodger, woefully unaccustomed either to personal success or inebriation, was so happy that his cheeks and collar were stained with tears.

He paused after explaining to me for the fifteenth time exactly how he'd taken his five wickets and looked around the bar with proprietorial pride.

'Good fwiends,' he sighed, waving his glass around airily and spilling a third of a pint of strong cider. 'These are all weal fwiends.'

Exhausted by this he leant back against the bar and carefully put his left elbow in a large puddle of beer. He didn't seem to notice.

Following his inspiration I looked around the room.

Arthur, our intemperate wicket keeper, was asleep or unconscious in a corner by the fire. Apart from his talent behind the stumps Arthur's most enviable skill is his ability to drift into unconsciousness while keeping his eyes open and looking as though he is still conscious and alert.

Those of us who know him well can tell Arthur's condition at a glance (the general rule is that if he isn't actually drinking and doesn't have a full container of some kind clutched in his fist then he is probably unconscious). The landlord of the Duck and Puddle was not, however, aware of Arthur's unnatural skill and he was busily telling our wicket keeper some long and complicated story about the local ironmonger, the local greengrocer's wife and a farming implement. The landlord seemed happy to accept Arthur's involuntary grunts as expressions of interest and encouragement to continue.

Young Simon, the teenage leg spinner, had fallen asleep over a letter he was writing to his mother. To celebrate his success with the ball Simon had been bought two pints of draught ale and the effect of the alcohol on his brain had been rapid.

Next to Simon sat Jerry Dixon and Brian O'Toole. Alcohol tends to make most people slightly more aggressive than usual but with Jerry this normal effect is reversed. After a few drinks Jerry becomes quiet and morose. He and Brian were deeply engaged in a depressing discussion about the illnesses they had both endured and the funerals they'd been to.

On the other side of the fireplace sat Norman, the vicar and June Tate.

No one had seen Sergeant Tate since the end of the match and on our return to the Duck and Puddle we had discovered that he had packed his bags, paid his bill and left. No one knew where he'd gone to and no-one, least of all June, seemed to care.

The vicar and the abandoned Mrs Tate were now sitting next to one another and giggling together like teenage lovers. The vicar had one hand on June Tate's knee and she seemed happy with this arrangement. They were both drinking gin and tonics.

Next to them Norman Wilkes seemed blissfully unaware of his gradual metamorphosis into a gooseberry. Norman is one of life's committed innocents; the sort of passive, wide eyed observer who believes what politicians say and always accepts the claims of advertisers and life insurance salesmen at face value. Norman's one brush with the law took place when he accepted as a client a brothel owner who managed to convince him that she was running a finishing school for young ladies. To Norman the burgeoning romance between Kurt and June was quite invisible. If he'd found them in bed together he would have readily accepted any protestations of innocence and any claims that they were really just 'good friends'.

That just left Oily.

Oily was draped over one end of the bar talking to the

brunette with the spectacular bust and the very short skirt. Their relationship had clearly long since developed into something more earthy than that of customer and barmaid. The barmaid's arms were resting on the counter and her more than ample bosom was resting on top of her folded arms. Oily's eyes were focussed on the centre of her deep and impressive cleavage which he clearly found understandably hypnotic. Every few moments one or the other of them would look at the bar clock slowly ticking its way towards contentment and delight. Oily had clearly forgotten all about Swansea and it seemed an unsuitable time to remind him of the past.

'Lets all have a glass of port!' said Wodger, suddenly. He levered himself up off the bar and stood unaided for a moment. 'To toast our success!' he said, lifting his glass and spilling what was left of his cider. Exhausted by this speech and physical activity he slumped down onto a bar stool and waved his empty glass in the direction of the blonde and unoccupied barmaid. She smiled at him, raised a carefully manicured eyebrow and lifted a bottle of port from the shelf behind her. Although she had been doing most of the work (her companion behind the counter had been far too busily occupied providing a feast for Oily's lecherous eyes) she seemed content.

Wodger peered at the bottle she was holding, as though examining a label he probably couldn't even see, and nodded in approval.

'A glass for everyone,' he told her, waving his empty glass around again to indicate that his generosity was not to be limited.

Drinking port always reminds me of a solicitor I used to know when I lived in London. He had a tremendous passion for good wines of all varieties but an especially strong passion for fine port. He was always going off to wine auctions and buying cases of the stuff to lay down in what he grandly called his 'cellars'. (The 'cellars' were in fact two lock up garages in Pinner).

I remember once going round to dinner just after he'd bought a whole case of 1945 port that an acquaintance of his had insisted was a tremendous bargain and an excellent investment.

He'd chilled a couple of bottles of decent white wine to

go with the trout and a couple of bottles of a well bred red to accompany the meat so by the time we'd got round to the bottle of fairly ordinary vintage port he'd brought out to be drunk with the stilton we were all much happier than we had been at the start of the meal. We were none of us incoherent or even noticeably unsteady but I don't think any of us would have been impressive at juggling or clay pigeon shooting.

We had got through no more than half a bottle of the cheap stuff when my solicitor friend suddenly got up from the table and disappeared from the dining room without a word. He came back a few minutes later carrying a dusty bottle with an almost indecipherable label. He carefully placed the bottle down in front of us with a gesture of generous triumph and undisguised pride.

'I thought you were keeping that as an investment?' said his wife, half in surprise, half in anger and half in anticipation.

'I was,' said the solicitor, with a smile. 'But I thought I'd just share a bottle with my good friends.' He waved an expansive hand around the table, produced fresh glasses and poured out generous measures of what turned out to be something prepared by angels from the breath of saints. 'After all,' he reassured himself, 'there's no real point in buying good wine unless you're prepared to drink it.'

'You're supposed to keep it for a special occasion,' his wife noted, slightly reprovingly.

'This *is* a special occasion,' announced the solicitor indignantly. 'We're drinking the 1945 port!' He paused and sipped at his glass. 'Anyway,' he added, 'it needed testing.'

These were arguments that no one was prepared to counter or determined to confound and so we drank a toast to celebrate the opening of the first bottle of our friend's 1945 port. Then, when the first bottle had gone, the solicitor brought up a second bottle so that we could drink a toast to the memory of the first bottle.

Having broken into the crate the solicitor's resolve disappeared like ice in warm gin and a week or so later his investment consisted of a wooden crate, twelve dusty but empty bottles and a number of very good friends who had all acquired a taste for fine but expensive port.

The port at the Duck and Puddle was hardly of the same vintage but it was received with distinct pleasure by everyone apart from Simon who was too firmly in the arms of Morpheus to acknowledge or take advantage of our captain's generosity. Arthur, our ancient and formidably pickled wicket keeper (who had woken automatically when the port was being distributed) selflessly drank Simon's measure for him.

*　　*　　*

All pleasures must be paid for, of course. And we learnt the price for our evening's conviviality when we awoke the following morning.

First, there was the bar bill. On our arrival at the Duck and Puddle we had rashly opened a 'team' bar bill to avoid the inconvenience of having to find cash before obtaining a drink. To say that the total startled us would not be an exaggeration. Norman burst into tears when he was told what his portion of the bill came to. Simon, already pale and sickly looking after the baptism of his liver, seemed close to collapse but was instantly rescued from embarrassment and possible penury by Oily who volunteered to pay his share of the bill as well as his own. Only Arthur seemed pleasantly surprised by the extent of his financial commitment. He seemed to regard the bill as modest and, indeed, compared to his normal expenditure on alcohol it probably was. (No one has ever known where Arthur's money comes from but the supply, like the contents of his hip flask, never seems to dry up).

But the price of our pleasure was not simply financial, of course. When the ten of us awoke the following morning we had nine hangovers between us. Only Arthur escaped this additional burden. He never gets hangovers since he never sobers up.

While the rest of us grimaced and winced at the sound of crunching toast and the hiss of roasting coffee beans Arthur simply tipped his head back and allowed the contents of his ever reliable flask to soothe and salve his wounded and much scarred spirit.

It was half past ten when we finally paid our bill, dragged our luggage out into the porch outside the pub and said farewell to the landlord. Brian O'Toole and I were the only ones to manage a full cooked breakfast. The rest of our touring party seemed satisfied with dry toast and black coffee. They consumed large quantities of both these staple ingredients of the touring cricketers diet.

Our destination was Bideford, just a few miles down the coast, where our second match was due to start that very afternoon, and Wodger was the first of our drivers to be prepared for the short journey. On his arrival at the Duck and Puddle Wodger's car had contained Sergeant Tate in the front seat and Norman and June Tate in the back seat. But Sergeant Tate was no longer with us, of course, and on his departure Wodger found that Norman was sitting next to him while June was joined in the back seat by the Revd Kurt Meitner.

At breakfast June and the vicar had been studiously careful to ignore one another. They had come down to the dining room separately and a casual observer would not have guessed that they had ever met before. It was this total absence of recognition which made it perfectly apparent to the rest of us that their romance had blossomed after Wodger's final round of port had brought our evenings celebrations to a close.

But by the time we were all ready to abandon the comfort of the Duck and Puddle they had either decided that such subterfuge was pointless or else they had found one another's physical attractions too powerful to ignore. When they got into the back of Wodger's motor car they put their arms around one another and snuggled up together as oblivious to observation as two lovers taking advantage of the darkness and anonymity of the back row of a cinema in an unfamiliar town.

Wodger seemed a little taken aback by this behaviour and sat bolt upright in the front of the car as though unaware of and disconnected from what was happening behind him.

Jerry and Brian were the next to leave and when their ancient Volvo had finally chugged out of sight I decided that I ought to try and find Oily, Arthur and Simon; none of whom were anywhere in sight.

Finding Arthur was easy. Even Dr Watson could have found Arthur – without the assistance of his famous companion. Arthur was in the bar, sitting next to the landlord (to whom we had all said our farewells just a few minutes earlier) and drinking whisky as though his life depended upon it, which, in a way, I suppose it did.

I left Arthur there while I looked for Simon and Oily.

Simon I found in his bedroom writing another letter to his mother.

And Oily found me in the corridor outside Simon's room.

'I've been looking for you!' he cried. 'Its time we left.' The brunette barmaid clung closely to him and had tears in her eyes. She was wearing a purple skirt that looked more like a pelmet and a tight, crocheted sweater that was at least five sizes too small for her. She tottered alongside Oily on slender four inch high heels and looking at her more closely I realised for the first time that she was much younger than she had first appeared.

Simon led the way, I followed and Oily brought up the rear with the buxom brunette barmaid.

Downstairs we picked up Arthur, said goodbye to the land-lord again and stuffed our bags into the boot of Oily's Jaguar. The blonde barmaid appeared and hugged and kissed us all and then Oily and I helped pour Arthur into the back of the car.

At this point I turned round tactfully so that Oily could say goodbye to the brunette barmaid.

'You coming?' I heard Oily call.

I turned back and to my astonishment saw that Oily was already settled in the driving seat. I looked around for the brunette but she was nowhere to be seen. Apart from myself the blonde barmaid was the only person around. With a strange feeling in the pit of my stomach I bent down and peered into the back of the car. There, squeezed in between Arthur and Simon was the brunette barmaid. She was smiling and crying at the same time and the purple pelmet around her waist had ridden up so far that Simon was blushing brightly and seemed to have no idea where to look. Arthur, sipping from his flask, did not seem to have noticed that we had acquired an extra passenger.

I opened my mouth to speak but could think of nothing sensible to say so I shut it again. Oily leant across the car and opened the front passenger door from the inside. I got in, fastened my seat belt and looked across at Oily. It was now clearly far too late to remind him of Swansea.

'Sharon's a cricket fan,' explained Oily as he let out the clutch and we moved noisily away from the Duck and Puddle, 'she's going to be our travelling spectator.'

I turned my head slightly and behind me could see that Sharon, who had managed to wriggle round so that she was kneeling on the back seat, was furiously waving her handkerchief at the rapidly disappearing blonde barmaid. Simon was unsuccessfully trying to ignore the fact that as Sharon waved her arm so her ample chest bobbed up and down just a few inches from his face.

My head was still throbbing from our evening's celebrations and I slumped back into the Jaguar's sumptuous leather and tried to sleep.

Behind me I could hear Arthur beginning to snore. It was good to know that there were at least some certainties in life.

* * *

CHAPTER FIVE

Our match at the Little Swell Cricket Club, just outside Bideford, was due to start at 2.00 pm precisely but at 1.45 pm precisely Oily, Arthur, Simon, Sharon and I were lost.

At the start of the tour Wodger had handed each one of us a photocopied itinerary which included details of all our opponents and notes on where we were due to stay at each venue.

'If you lose your way or get separated from the rest of the team,' Wodger explained, 'all you have to do is make your own way to the next village or pub on the list.'

In principle it sounded sensible. In practice there was a snag. Neither Oily nor I knew the faintest thing about navigation.

The only map we had was printed in the back of Oily's diary and the whole of the West of England was crammed onto six square inches of endpaper. The scale of the map was such that Oily's thumbnail covered the entire distance between Lynton (the nearest proper town to Queens Lapford) and Bideford (the nearest important place to Little Swell). Finding Bideford was easy. Finding Little Swell was hard.

We had been lucky on our first day's journey. The main road from the motorway had taken us straight into Lynton and Queens Lapford had been signposted from the centre of the village.

We were not so lucky in Bideford.

As we drove around Bideford in eccentric circles Oily turned to Sharon for help. But she was as lost as we were. It turned out that she'd never been further West than Barnstaple in her life.

It was luck rather than skill, judgement or experience which eventually took us through the village of Little Swell and right past the cricket ground where the Little Swell team played its matches. We arrived with less than five minutes to spare and found Wodger in a desperate state of excitement. He'd managed to borrow one spare player from the home team (June Tate's emergence as a player had brought us up to a full complement of eleven players but her husband's disappearance had taken us back to ten players again) but did not expect to find it so easy to obtain another four players on loan.

Wodger had already lost the toss but, in view of our absence, the opposing captain had generously agreed to take the field in the hope that we would arrive in time to bat.

Wodger and Norman opened the batting while Oily, Arthur, Simon and I got changed. Sharon, who refused to be parted from Oily, came into the dressing room with us and sat in a corner brushing her hair. I couldn't get over how Sharon had changed. While serving behind the bar she'd seemed confident and mature. Now, away from what was obviously her more natural habitat, she seemed shy, immature and uncomfortable.

As soon as we'd changed we joined the rest of the team who were sprawled untidily on the grass in front of the pavilion. Jerry, never couth at the best of times, had taken off his shirt to soak up the glorious August sunshine. I never failed to be astonished at the extent of his tattoos.

I've lost count of the number of village cricket grounds I've seen or played on but the Little Swell ground was one of the most remarkable and unusual I've ever come across. The centre of the ground, where the wickets are pitched, is shaped rather like a saucer with the result that bowlers at both ends are always running downhill.

The climb up the sides of the saucer is at its steepest directly behind the two wickets where it rises upwards for about thirty yards before reaching twin peaks and sloping back down towards the boundary markings which run a yard or so inside a thick blackthorn and hawthorn hedge.

The result is that players who field on the boundary directly behind the bowler or the wicket keeper are totally invisible to the batsmen. The effect of this is to lull the batsmen into a false sense of security when hitting out or running between the wickets.

Norman was the first to discover the unique danger of batting at Little Swell.

The third ball he received was short, slow medium pace and pitched about six inches outside the off stump. Norman is not quick footed but he had plenty of time to drive the ball straight back down the wicket, straight past the despairing hand of the bowler, over the hill and apparently on over the boundary for six.

Norman was walking down the wicket to receive the congratulations of his captain when a tall, blonde haired, grinning fielder suddenly appeared holding the ball in an outstretched arm.

Norman looked at the fielder in astonishment. Open mouthed he looked at Wodger as though for some sort of explanation. Wodger seemed as puzzled as he was so Norman turned to the bowler who had a big smile on his face and his arms outstretched in appeal.

'How was that?' shouted the bowler, making it clear that he was in absolutely no doubt.

The umpire, raising a nicotine stained and slightly arthritic index finger, made his decision known.

'Where did he come from?' asked Norman, a man who is normally so meek mannered that when he bowls someone else has to do his appealing for him.

'Long-off,' answered the bowler.

'I didn't know he was there!' protested Norman.

'It's up to the batsman to acquaint himself with the bowler's field placing,' said the umpire in a gruff and slightly reproving voice. He tapped two counting coins together slightly impatiently.

Wodger moved a little closer to Norman and put a hand on his shoulder. He shrugged, sharing Norman's frustration but not knowing what else he could do.

Sadly and slowly Norman turned away and dragged his bat back towards the pavilion. The journey always seems much longer when you've scored a duck.

As he walked towards us and Jerry put his shirt on, fastened up his pads and looked around for his bat Oily leant across to me and whispered in my ear.

'How do we know that he actually *caught* it?' he asked.

I looked at him in horror since such an awful thought had not even entered my mind.

Oily shrugged. 'Just a thought.'

Jerry was the next to discover the very natural hazards of batting at Little Swell.

Normally Jerry is as aggressive as a batsman as he is at everything else he does. But he began his innings at Little Swell with caution.

After four overs he and Wodger had scored just three runs between them – all 'stolen' after nudges in the direction of mid wicket or cover point. Outside the actual square at Little Swell the outfield was rather long and balls travelled slowly on their uphill journey through lush grass.

At the beginning of the next over, however, the Little Swell opening bowler sent down a ball that was noticeably quicker than anything else he'd bowled. It was slightly wide of the leg stump.

Jerry tried to sweep the ball towards the square leg boundary, mistimed and sent the ball sizzling through a space where leg slip would have been fielding if there had been a leg slip. The wicket keeper was slow to respond but I doubt if he would have been able to reach the ball even if he had moved with more speed.

'Yes!' cried Wodger, realising that there were no fielders behind the wicket keeper and watching with amusement as two bulky slips lumbered hopelessly after the ball.

Jerry didn't need telling twice. He shot out of his crease like a greyhound spotting a hare.

They had run one, were about to complete a second and were clearly intending to take at least a third and maybe a fourth run when the ball suddenly appeared back over the brow of the hill behind the wicket keeper travelling at an incredible speed and fired into the wicket keepers hands with enviable accuracy. The two slip fielders, still in sight, had both turned to watch the ball arrive in the wicket keepers gloves and they were chuckling with accustomed delight.

'Owzat?' cried the wicket keeper removing the bails with Jerry still two yards out of his crease.

Jerry, who had a moment earlier been wondering whether he and Wodger would be able to run five before the slip fielders caught up with the ball, couldn't believe his eyes. He put his head down, grounded his bat and raced for the line as though his life depended upon it.

The wicket keeper didn't help things at all.

When Jerry, breathless from a combination of exhaustion, frustration and anger, finally came to a halt several yards past the stumps he threw his bat down, put both gloved hands on his hips and scowled at the wicket keeper.

Lesser men would have quailed but the wicket keeper was not a lesser man. He was a traffic warden and part time fireman and he knew what was right.

'You're out!' he told Jerry with accurate but undiplomatic simplicity. He pointed down the wicket to the umpire whose digital callisthenics gave full support to this allegation.

'But ...?' spluttered Jerry, waving airily in the direction from which the ball had come. 'Who ... where ... how?'

The wicket keeper pointed to a small figure who had climbed up to the brow of the hill and was now looking down at the scattered stumps and bails with undisguised delight. 'Him!' he answered unnecessarily.

There is no knowing what Jerry's next response might or might not have been had not Wodger wandered down the wicket and used his modest talents as a peace-maker to prevent bloodshed. When he stamped past us and strode back into the pavilion Jerry's face was as black as a sweep's and far less jovial. We winced as we heard Jerry hitting things with his bat as he strode around our tiny dressing room.

After that, of course, our batsmen lost their nerve completely. No one dared to hit a ball out of the saucer because no one knew where there were likely to be any fielders. Even when a ball did escape the clutches of the close in fielders and accidentally disappear over the brows of the two main hills, no one dared to run.

Before the match started it had been agreed that each innings would be limited to twenty five overs but by the time our allocation had gone we had scored just 47 runs and lost only five wickets. It was a dismal and depressing performance.

'Never mind,' said Wodger, replete with forced joviality

as we nibbled at cucumber sandwiches and slices of fruit cake provided by the home side's catering team, 'two can play at that game.'

It seemed a not unreasonable assertion but in practice Wodger's optimism proved unsustainable.

Right from the start Wodger put four men out on the boundary – all out of sight of the home side's opening batsmen. Simon and I patrolled one hidden boundary while Oily and Norman patrolled the other.

We didn't see the ball at all for the first three quarters of an hour. The home side's batsmen scored at a sparkling rate – hitting every loose ball straight through to the square leg and cover boundaries. The few members of our side who could see what was going on were completely unable to quell the onslaught.

After forty five minutes a badly hit shot sent the ball straight back past the bowler and into my territory. I only saw it when my attention was attracted by shouts from the distant unknown and when I picked up the ball I had no idea where to throw it. Eventually I took pot luck and hurled it in to where I thought the stumps ought to be. It turned out later that I'd thrown the ball straight past cover point. They got an extra two runs from my throw.

After an hour, with the home side needing just ten to win, Wodger brought us all into view though whether this was so that we could take part in the match or watch the final throes of the annihilation I'm not sure. Their opening pair were still together and our bowlers were all demoralised.

The inevitable happened, of course.

With no one fielding at long on or long off the batsmen took every opportunity to drive the ball straight back past the bowler. And with no one at third man or long leg every snick past the wicket keeper brought a fat reward.

The match finished a few minutes later with the home side having ten wickets and eight overs to spare.

We left Little Swell with heavy hearts. Rightly or wrongly we felt that we'd been cheated.

The home side were delighted by their victory and invited us to celebrate with them in their local inn. But Wodger, speaking on our behalf and anxious to get as much distance between

Jerry and their team as possible, declined politely.

*　　*　　*

Because the only pub in Little Swell did not have any rooms to let Wodger had booked us all in at the Bat and Belfry in Bideford. It was about half past eight that evening when we arrived and the general air of gloom and despondency which hung over the team matched the atmosphere in the hostelry. A long list of rules and regulations hung threateningly next to the receptionists desk and the only member of staff visible was a small, ferret faced man who greeted us with a warning that any damage to fixtures or fittings would have to be paid for. The inside of the pub was painted dark brown and this, combined with the fact that the lighting in the reception area and main staircase was provided by a single 60 watt light bulb, meant that it was difficult to appreciate the quality of the fixtures and fittings which we had been advised to respect.

After abandoning our luggage in our small, dreary, ill lit bedrooms we met in the small, dreary, ill lit bar where the small, ferret faced man responded to our requests for food with a startled, slightly offended, look that might have been more appropriate if we had asked him to provide us with a dozen geisha girls.

'Food?' he said, daring us to repeat our request.

'Something simple will do,' Jerry assured him. 'Egg and chips.'

'I've got crisps,' said ferret face. 'Prawn and cucumber, liver and kidney or garlic and onion.' He reached behind him, rummaged around in a large cardboard box and produced a handful of crisp packets.

Bideford is not well endowed with good eating establishments. Or if it is then the establishments it has hide themselves away from travellers. We must have walked along every street in the town in search of a cafe or restaurant. By nine thirty we would have happily eaten anything other than liver and kidney crisps. A plateful of stale cheese sandwiches would have drawn gasps of delight from our starving mouths. A few bowlfuls of tinned vegetable soup would have had us writing letters of recommendation to the Good Restaurant

Guide.

At ten we found a chip shop that was just about to close. The owners, a huge, worried looking man and his petite, nervous wife seemed alarmed by our presence in their shop.

'Could I have cod and chips eleven times, please,' said Wodger. 'We'll put our own salt and vinegar on.'

'Cod?' repeated the chip shop proprietor, He looked at his wife for encouragement.

'And chips?' she said, timidly.

Wodger repeated our order and Oily inspired a little activity by producing a handful of bank notes from his trouser pocket.

Fifteen minutes later we took proud possession of eleven portions of the tastiest, most beautifully battered, most exquisitely fried cod ever served outside Yorkshire and eleven portions of the hottest, most evenly textured and perfectly cooked chips ever served.

Unwilling to return to the Bats in the Belfry we strolled about the deserted streets of Bideford clutching our packets of cod and chips and doing our best to cheer one another up.

'Have you heard from your husband?' Jerry asked June.

June, her mouth full of chips, shook her head and moved away from the vicar's side.

'Funny,' persisted Jerry, 'him just going off like that.'

June and the vicar moved still further apart. They both looked distinctly uncomfortable.

'Rotten luck, you getting run out like that,' said Wodger to Jerry, anxious to change the subject and spare June and the vicar any further embarrassment.

Jerry tried to say something but half choked on a piece of fish.

'You'd be amazed at the number of people who choke to death,' said Brian, cautiously nibbling at a chip. 'I wonder if these were cooked in vegetable oil?'

'How are you enjoying being away from home?' Norman asked Simon.

Simon swallowed hard and looked down at the pavement.

'I suppose you get a bit homesick, eh?' persisted Norman.

Simon rubbed a sleeve across his face too late to stop a tear falling onto his chips.

'I hope the other places you've booked us into are better than the Bat and Belfry,' Oily said to Wodger. 'Bit miserable isn't it?'

'I'm sorry . . .' Wodger apologised. He waved his arms about and scattered half a dozen chips onto the pavement.

'How's Sharon enjoying the trip?' I asked Oily. He glowered at me. We both turned slightly and watched her as she stumbled along the pavement, restricted by her tight skirt and constantly struggling to maintain her balance as her slender heels click clacked across the uneven paving slabs. She seemed to get younger and younger. She looked up, saw us watching and waved a chip in our direction and tried to smile. She blew Oily a kiss but suddenly looked alone and vulnerable. I felt sorry for her.

Glumly and slowly we meandered through the streets of Bideford until tiredness and the coolness of the summer evening prepared us for our dark and gloomy rooms at the Bat and Belfry.

'Has anyone seen Arthur?' asked the vicar as we waited for the ferret faced man to open up the front door and let us in.

'Not since the chip shop,' said Norman. 'He was with us there.'

'Arthur will be all right,' Wodger reassured us. 'Arthur is always all right.'

Arthur was all right. He was stretched out unconscious across two uncomfortable looking seats in the Bat and Belfry public bar. Oily and I gently picked him up and carried him upstairs to bed.

'Never mind,' said Wodger, struggling to find a ray of optimism with which to scatter the dark clouds which had dominated the day, 'there's always tomorrow.'

*   *   *

CHAPTER SIX

When I awoke the following morning, the fourth full day of our tour, I felt wonderful. I had slept well and felt refreshed and ready for another cricket match. The sunshine was already filtering through the thin, unlined curtains of my bedroom and the motes of dust which danced in the beams of morning brightness seemed full of joy. The room was full of old fashioned furniture and had a faded look about it but all this seemed quite right and had I had the power I would not have changed a thing about it. Modern hotel bedrooms have a sameness, a dullness, a safe predictability about them which deadens the senses and numbs the mind.

Brimming with the joys of summer I leapt from my bed and wandered into the adjoining bathroom where I bathed in a huge, white enamelled cast iron tub with massive brass taps and an ingenious drainage apparatus and shaved my reflection in an ornate brass bordered mirror.

Breakfast was served in a room we hadn't seen before; a huge, panelled dining room which was dominated by a long, bare, oak dining table.

Along the whole of one side of the room a series of sideboards groaned under the combined weight of a dozen silverplate serving dishes, each one protected by one of those delightfully old fashioned shiny silver lids. There were rashers of bacon, some streaky, some less so, some simply cooked, some crisp; sausages of every imaginable size and shape; eggs scrambled, eggs poached and eggs fried; there were tomatoes and mushrooms, there were racks of toast and pots of piping hot coffee and tea.

Of the ferret faced man from the night before there was no sign at all. In his place there now appeared a small, well dressed rather dapper little man who, working apparently alone, kept the dishes on the sideboards full. Only the pencil line moustache betrayed the fact that our considerate host of the morning and our less than welcoming host of the previous night were one and the same person.

Oily said he thought that perhaps the fellow was a breakfast man, unsuited to evening time frolicking and feasting. I said I thought that perhaps now that he knew us better and was assured that we were not the sort of people to damage fixtures and fittings he felt more comfortable in our presence.

Strengthened and invigorated by a night's sleep and a good breakfast, but most of all by the realisation that we had a new match to play and could forget our dismal experience at Little Swell, we set off down the North Devon coast towards North Cornwall, Bude and our third fixture.

Anxious to arrive on time for this fixture both Jerry and Oily chose to follow Wodger in close convoy. Wodger, we discovered, had taken the precaution of stocking his car with copies of a complete set of West Country Ordnance Survey maps. Name a beacon, a disused church, a milestone or a cattle grid and Wodger could pinpoint it to within a yard. He had acquired a gentle familiarity with every contour line, every fence, every copse and every public house west of Somerset. A friend of mine swears that if you sit still long enough while they're making one of those maps you're likely to find yourself marked down alongside other landmarks and points of local interest.

We arrived at the site of our next match, Combe Regis Cricket Ground, at 11.30 am; parked our cars and were delighted to see that the ground was flat; no mounds, no hills, no dips, no hollows, nowhere for fielders to hide in wait.

We had not booked rooms in Combe Regis because the local cricket team fixture secretary had insisted that his team members would be delighted to offer us hospitality for the night. Normally none of us are too keen on this sort of arrangement. We prefer to pay our own way and retain our independence. Staying the night with cricketers against whom you've just played a match can be fraught with danger and embarrassment. But the Combe Regis secretary had insisted and Wodger said that it would have been rude to refuse his offer of hospitality.

And so with nowhere in particular to go we sprawled on the grass and enjoyed the gentle sunshine.

We'd been there for about twenty minutes when we heard what sounded rather like a herd of stampeding buffalo. Its remarkable how well sounds are transmitted through the earth and lying flat on our backs in the sunshine we all heard it.

It was Norman who spotted them first. There were about a dozen of them, dressed in matching blue tracksuits with the name of the cricket club emblazoned on both front and back. They were jogging along a nearby track and as they thundered past we could see that they all looked remarkably fit and in good condition. One or two looked slightly red faced but there was no puffing or wheezing. These, we realised with some alarm, were our next opponents.

As they disappeared over the horizon we looked at one another silently.

It was Oily who broke the spell.

'I don't have much faith in all that fitness nonsense,' he announced defiantly. 'Wears you out.'

I knew what Oily meant. He and I had tried it once.

It was before either of us were married. We'd decided one summer that instead of going away on holiday to have fun we ought to try and better ourselves. At the time everyone was doing it. You could go away on holidays where they gave you computer problems to solve from seven in the morning until nine at night or you could spend a month pony trekking through the Himalayas in an attempt to find yourself. The more money you'd got the worse the conditions you could afford to buy yourself. One couple I knew, who had spent a fortune on gadgets for their kitchen, had spent another small fortune on a holiday in Africa where they'd had to put up with facilities which they wouldn't have dreamt of tolerating if they'd been at home.

After looking at a pile of brochures Oily and I had decided to go away on a golfing holiday abroad. The brochure promised that we'd be able to reduce our handicaps, learn to play better golf and enjoy ourselves at the same time. It sounded irresistible.

We realised we had made a mistake on our first morning when, at about half past six, we were woken up by a chap in a pair of white shorts and a red vest who turned out to be the hotel's own resident assistant professional. He seemed awfully cheery and disgustingly full of beans for the time of morning but we thought we ought to show willing so we staggered down into the hotel lobby where we met all our fellow holiday-makers. There were about forty of us altogether; including would be golf champions from Germany, France and Sweden.

When he was satisfied that everyone was present the young professional led us all out of the hotel and down onto the beach. There, under the early morning sun, he gave us a pep talk, telling us that a good golfer needs to be in superb physical shape and assuring us that all the top professionals went through the exercise routine he was going to show us.

He then got us doing all sorts of bizarre and painful things, exercising muscles which had lain idle for years.

After forty painful minutes he led us along to a beach cafe where we had a snack of natural yoghurt, bran and orange juice. We were allowed ten minutes for this before we led back out onto the beach for a jogging session.

Oily and I found it all rather hard going and we tried to stop and take a break several times but every time we slowed down the professional would come back and shout at us. He was a meaty looking fellow, with muscles bulging through his cut off shirt, and he got quite nasty when we moaned so we tried to show willing.

The jogging stopped at about half past nine and Oily and I were looking forward to breakfast but it turned out that we'd already had that. We were given a drink of weak decaffeinated coffee and then led down to the hotel's own driving range where the senior professional and another assistant proceeded to show us why we were all terrible golfers. The first assistant, the muscular hunk who'd had us grunting through our callisthenics on the beach, disappeared and Oily and I suspected that he'd gone off for a proper cooked breakfast and a snooze.

By the time we were allowed out of the driving range at one

o'clock we both had blisters on our hands and we were looking forward to a dip in the hotel swimming pool and a quiet afternoon's sunbathing. We'd noticed that there were some very nice samples of bikini material being modelled around the bar.

But there wasn't any time for swimming, sunbathing or ogling. After a lunch which consisted of thirty calories worth of lettuce and tomato we were hauled out of the dining room and dumped on the golf course where we were told that we were to take part in a fourball competition. We had to play with partners who'd been allocated to us and I found myself playing with a German and two Swedes. Oily was allowed to play with two Swedes and a German. One of Oily's partners spoke a little English but none of mine did and my German is about as good as my Swedish.

The competition finished at six. Dinner, which consisted almost exclusively of small pieces of octopus, finished at seven thirty. After that we all had to go along to the lecture theatre where one of the assistant professionals gave us a two hour illustrated lecture on aerodynamic club stress and the problems of turf maintenance in hot climates. The bulk of the lecture was in Portuguese.

It was announced at nine thirty that we could have the rest of the day to ourselves and for a few moments Oily and I shared a burst of mild optimism. But then the professional told us that he recommended an early night because the next morning's exercises were planned to start at six. Apparently they'd started late on our first morning so that we could have a bit of a lie in after our flight.

We stuck it for three days and the routine didn't change at all. Not surprisingly, we decided that it was all too much for us and that we didn't want to play golf that well after all. We escaped to the airport at five o'clock one morning and bought single tickets back to London. We didn't dare go back home because we'd told everyone where we were going and what we were doing so we spent the rest of the fortnight hiding in a small boarding house just outside Slough. When we finally got home no one could understand why we weren't suntanned. Neither of us played golf for six months afterwards.

*   *   *

Within minutes our prospective opponents were out of sight so we closed our eyes and lay back to soak up a little more sunshine. Doing nothing is an undervalued skill; it's something they should teach children.

We slept and rested for an hour or so, watching small, fluffy white clouds drift aimlessly across the sky, making daisy chains and watching butterflies dance around unpredictably. The only noise was the sound of buttercups bursting into blossom.

The silence, the peace and the stillness were eventually broken by Jerry. 'What about some lunch?' he asked, suddenly sitting up.

'I'm comfortable here,' said Brian. 'But I'm hungry.'

'Lets have a picnic,' suggested Sharon. 'I like picnics.'

'Great idea,' said Simon.

'Slight snag,' said Wodger.

We all looked at him.

'We haven't got anything to eat,' he explained.

'We passed a small shop about a mile back,' said June Tate.

Wodger stood up and got out his car keys, 'Come on, then,' he said to her. 'Let's go and get some food.'

'I'll come,' said Sharon, standing up and straightening her clothes. Today she was wearing a lime green pelmet. It made an interesting contrast with her bright orange sweater.

I love picnics too – especially impromptu ones.

When I first got married we often used to have wonderful picnics. We used to have a small, old fashioned wooden sided Morris Minor and we'd go out for the day with a loaf of French style bread fresh from the local baker's carried in an old fashioned wicker shopping basket together with a large chunk of cheese, a pot of pâté and a bottle of something tasty. We took two drinking glasses with us but never bothered with plates. The only cutlery we took was my Swiss Army penknife – we used the large blade for cutting the bread and the small blade for slicing up the cheese and spreading the pâté.

Then, one Christmas, a friend of ours who knew that we enjoyed picnicking bought us a neat, wickerwork basket which contained a set of matching blue plastic plates, half a dozen cups and saucers, a thermos flask, six blue plastic beakers, six blue plastic knives, six blue plastic forks, six blue plastic teaspoons and six blue plastic dessert spoons. There was even a cruet set made out of blue plastic.

It was a very well made picnic basket but it didn't have any room in it for food so we still had to take our old fashioned shopping basket as well.

Then someone else bought us a special wicker basket designed for carrying a bottle and half a dozen drinking glasses. It had very smart leather straps to prevent the bottle and glasses from breaking.

By this time our picnics were becoming rather complicated affairs and friends, getting the mistaken impression that we rather liked to do things in style, bought us all sorts of other bits and pieces of picnic ephemera. My wife's aunt bought us a lovely blue Irish linen tablecloth and four matching napkins while my wife's sister got us four beautifully engraved silver napkin rings.

My grandmother bought us a little gas stove for our anniversary and my brother and his wife gave us two folding chairs with weatherproof double thickness nylon seats and specially structured aluminium struts. A cousin of my mother's gave us a tiny travelling pewter mustard pot with a little lid that fastened down with the aid of a tricky little catch that could only be fastened with the aid of a pair of eyebrow tweezers.

Some people we met while on holiday in the Lake District were so impressed by our picnic equipment that they sent us a windbreak for Christmas and my sister's parents in law made a tremendous fuss of presenting us with a groundsheet which had a lovely tartan pattern on both sides. One side was Campbell and the other side was McLeod. A friend I was at University with sent us a portable toilet, complete with bucket, tent and spade and a girl friend of my wife's sent us a boxed set of assorted insect repellants. Until then I didn't even know that there was anyone out there making boxed sets of insect repellents. Its daunting to think that there are grown men who earn a living out of making and selling such things.

Although all these bits and pieces of impedimenta were undoubtedly intended to make picnicking easier and more comfortable they had the opposite effect. They made picnics unbearably complicated.

Instead of just being able to throw some food into a bag whenever the weather looked fine we had to plan days ahead and start packing before we knew what the weather was going to be like. If we wanted to go out into the country on a Sunday afternoon we had to sort out all the things we wanted to take with us on the Tuesday or the Wednesday at the latest. Then we had to get a refill for the gas stove and wash the plastic cutlery (which, however good our intentions may have been, always seemed to get forgotten and put away smeared with mustard) and freeze the coolers for the ice bag.

Altogether, it took a good three or four days to get ready for a picnic and so we could never be quite sure whether to plan for sunshine or for a cold wind. To cope with this uncertainty we bought a massive umbrella and table so that if it was wet we could still picnic comfortably. We also bought fur linked anoraks for ourselves on the grounds that our picnics took so much planning that they couldn't just be abandoned because of bad weather.

Eventually picnicking became such a fearful chore that we lost interest. All the pleasure had gone out of it and none of the effort seemed really worthwhile. Every now and again our friends and relatives would ask us why we didn't go out on picnics any more and we'd have to ahem and cough and change the subject quickly.

Less than a quarter of an hour after they'd left June, Sharon and Wodger returned with two plastic carrier bags full of food. They'd got bread, Cheddar cheese, Cheshire cheese, double Gloucester cheese, a couple of pound of apples, and a large jar of pickled onions. The boot of Wodger's car was packed with cardboard boxes containing bottles of cider, bottles of lemonade and cans of lager.

'We haven't got any plates or glasses,' said June.

The general view was that this did not matter in the slightest.

'We haven't got a knife to cut the bread and the cheese,' said Wodger.

'We have!' I announced quickly. 'My Swiss Army penknife will do just fine.' I took it out of my pocket with a proud flourish and handed it to June. 'Use the large blade for the bread and the small blade for the cheese,' I told her.

*   *   *

CHAPTER SEVEN

Captaincy at club cricket level is a very different matter to captaincy in the professional game. Indeed I would claim that of the two, professional captains have things easy. They know that on the day of the match all their eleven players will turn up, on time and properly kitted out. They don't have to worry about losing their wicket keeper because his wife's relatives have suddenly turned up or because the bathroom shelf has come loose. They don't have to worry about their star opening batsman going to the wrong ground. They never wake up in the morning and find that three of their regular players have decided to take their summer holidays right in the middle of the season. They never lose four players when someone's ancient Ford Escort breaks down on the bypass. They never get to a match and find all their players suffering from wicked hangovers. They never have to try and sort out a sticking ballcock in the only lavatory or lend someone's girlfriend money to buy bread and cheese for sandwiches. They never have to worry about players who turn up with no cricket whites or boots.

And they never have to tour with ten players when eleven would be regarded by most captains as the absolute minimum. Touring with a player short is something of a nightmare for any captain. When the Combe Regis team turned up, at about half past one, Wodger's first task was to ask their captain if they could spare a player.

The Combe Regis captain, a tall, slender fellow with no chin, no hair and very little natural charm, looked down his nose at Wodger and shook his head.

'I don't think that would be right,' he announced, apparently offended by this request. 'One can't see the England captain asking his Australian counterpart to lend a player, can one?'

He actually used the word 'counterpart'!

Wodger looked rather guilty and embarrassed, like a head boy being told off by the headmaster. He muttered something apologetic and backed away.

'We'll have to play with ten men,' he told us, gloomily.

No one said anything. We knew from past experience that although it may not sound like much of a handicap playing with ten men means almost certain defeat. However weak the eleventh player is his presence invariably makes a massive difference to the team's morale as well as to its fielding and batting prospects.

'What about Sharon?'

We all looked around to see who had spoken. It was Simon. He spoke so rarely that at first no one had recognised his voice.

There was a long and probably significant silence.

It was Jerry who broke it.

'Sharon?' he said.

Simon said nothing but went bright red with embarrassment.

'Seems a good idea to me,' said Brian. 'We've already got one woman playing. And she's done all right for us so far.'

'I don't think we have a lot of choice.' said Wodger with unexpected firmness. 'I think its a splendid idea.' He paused and looked around. 'Does anyone know where she is?'

We found her sitting in Oily's car, using the driving mirror to help her perform heavy structural work on her eyelashes.

She seemed startled when Wodger opened the front passenger door and peered in at her. He must have looked like the leader of a lynching party with half a dozen of us crowded round behind him.

'Sharon, would you do us a favour, please?' asked Wodger, politely. 'Would you play for our team today?'

It would be an understatement to say that Sharon looked surprised. I think that she would have probably been no more startled if the Prime Minister had turned up and asked her to join the Cabinet. She lowered her hand, opened her mouth

55

and turned and blinked at Wodger. She looked around and eventually spied the person she was looking for.

'Me?' she asked Oily.

Oily smiled at her and nodded.

We all smiled at her and nodded. It must have been a terrifying sight.

'I can't play cricket,' Sharon protested, as though suddenly remembering this complication.

'Thats all right,' Wodger assured her. 'Bit of fielding and a bit of batting – that's all.'

'If you don't play we're a man short,' said Jerry ungallantly.

This simple honesty seemed to make sense to Sharon. 'OK, then,' she said. She opened the driver's door and clambered out of the car. She was wearing a pair of skin tight turquoise trousers and a lilac T shirt that was several sizes too small for her. As usual she was balancing on pencil thin heels that sank into the turf every time she tried to walk.

'Great idea, Simon!' said Wodger, with a broad grin. 'It was Simon's idea,' he told Sharon across the Jaguar roof.

Sharon looked across at Simon and smiled. Simon blushed violently until his cheeks were as red as a new cricket ball.

'We must find you some gear,' Wodger told Sharon. He delegated this task to Oily, Jane and the vicar and hurried off to join the Combe Regis captain who, smartly turned out in a blue blazer with an MCC badge on the pocket, was standing impatiently on the edge of the pitch waiting to toss a coin to see who would bat first.

It was no surprise to anyone when we heard that Wodger had lost the toss and that we would be batting first. Three minutes later Norman and our gentle captain stepped out onto the pitch together and walked out to the middle.

Wodger took guard and we all watched in silent horror as their opening bowler, a huge chap with a massive, drooping moustache, walked back thirty paces to begin his run up. Lots of bowlers have long, meandering run ups designed to convince batsmen that they are going to bowl fast but this player's walk back to his mark looked distinctly serious.

Thirty seconds later we all realised just how serious he was when his first ball clipped Wodger's off stump and sent both stump and bails cartwheeling backwards towards the wicket-keeper long before Wodger had even begun to play a stroke.

'Howzzzzzzzzaaaaaaaaaaaaaaaaaarrrrrrrrrrttt?' demanded the bowler unnecessarily. He'd ended up standing about two yards in front of Wodger.

'No ball!' shouted the umpire simultaneously, stretching an arm into the air and turning towards the scorer's table.

'What?' demanded the bowler, turning and staring at the umpire. Even from the boundary edge his glower looked intimidating.

But the umpire stood his ground.

He was a tiny little chap who didn't look as though he'd ever have the nerve to say 'boo' to a duck let alone a goose. But although he flinched he didn't look in the slightest bit inclined to alter his decision.

The bowler stood still and silent for what seemed to be an eternity then slowly started to walk back to his mark again.

His second ball was, if anything, even faster than the first.

Once again Wodger had not moved when the ball pitched a yard or so in front of him. But this time the ball clipped the edge of his bat and shot off through the slips to the boundary.

The umpire signalled a four. The bowler's fury increased.

By the end of the over Wodger had survived two lbw appeals and had scored another two boundaries.

It was an unsteady but useful start.

Wodger's luck continued for another two overs until he lifted a delivery from the other opening bowler high into the sky over mid on. The fielder circled underneath it for what seemed like a lifetime and then took a splendid, well judged catch.

We were 28 for 1 and even Wodger, when he returned to the safety of the pavilion steps, admitted that he had been 'rather lucky'.

By the time I went in to bat we had survived about a dozen close appeals, scored 57 runs and lost four wickets. It hadn't escaped our notice that all the dismissals had been sanctioned by just one of the umpires. The tiny little chap who'd 'no-balled' the Combe Regis star opening bowler's first ball still hadn't accepted a single appeal. We were, however, comforted by the knowledge that *both* the umpires had been provided by the Combe Regis side. No one could possibly accuse us of anything underhand.

Sadly I did not share in the team's good fortune. The first ball I received pitched on or just outside my off stump, broke viciously off the seam, somehow managed to find a space between my bat and my pads and neatly removed my leg bail. I looked down the wicket but the umpire, a plump, rosy cheeked, cheery looking fellow seemed perfectly well satisfied that the bowler had not broken any existing regulations.

Walking back to the pavilion after being dismissed is always something of a problem for me. I never quite know where to look. If I've scored a few runs I want to go slowly, to bathe in the applause of my team mates and any spectators who happen to be there. But do I wave my bat, raise my cap or wave a hand in modest appreciation of this earned approbation? Or, as so many professional batsmen do, should I simply hang my head and trudge homewards as though dissatisfied with my own performance?

Failing to score at all makes the walk back to the pavilion particularly difficult. Ideally, I think there ought to be a set of steps near every wicket and an underground tunnel back to the pavilion for the exclusive use of batsmen who've been dismissed for nought.

But there is, of course, no such escape. The walk back always seems at least twice as long as the walk out. And I don't know which are worse – the looks of pitying sympathy one gets from ones team-mates or the looks of ill-disguised disgust and contempt which adorn the faces of the deckchair spectators.

Gloomily I threw my bat down on the grass and sat down beside Norman and Oily.

'Rotten luck,' said Norman.

'Terrible luck,' added Oily. 'Unplayable ball.'

'It happens,' I said, philosophically, as though it didn't really matter.

My short innings seemed to mark a downturn in the team's luck. Brian was caught at mid on, the vicar was bowled round his legs and Arthur trod on his wicket trying to evade a short pitched ball which seemed to be aimed straight at his throat. When Simon gave a straightforward return catch to the

Combe Regis captain we had scored 72 for 9 and our only hope was that Sharon, due to join June at the wicket, would launch her cricketing career in as spectacular way as June had a couple of days earlier.

Sharon's appearance as she went out ot bat did not encourage confidence.

She wore a white short sleeved sweater belonging to Oily, a pair of white tennis shorts belonging to the vicar and Brian's batting pads which were the only ones small enough to fit her. No one had any boots to fit her and so she had to wear a pair of her own extremely high heeled shoes which Oily had carefully covered with white polish especially for the occasion. Her progress as she walked out to the wicket was slow but undoubtedly eye catching. The opposition were so startled by her appearance that no one thought to complain about her wearing high heels on the batting strip.

I don't know whether it was a result of instructions from the captain or not but the fielders crowded around her enthusiastically. As she bent over her bat (borrowed from Brian) the two silly-points and the silly mid-off seemed to think it necessary to move even closer and so they halted the bowler in his tracks while they edged forwards a few feet. Behind Sharon backward short-leg, short-leg, forward short-leg and silly mid-on all edged forwards a few feet too. By the time they were satisfied with their positions any one of them could have reached out and touched Sharon (and it was fairly clear that all of them would have liked to).

'Reminds me of a girl I once took to the golf course,' said Oily, turning to me with a broad grin on his face. He didn't seem to mind in the slightest that Sharon was the subject of so much attention. 'A cousin of mine,' he added.

I should perhaps explain that Oily has rather more cousins than anyone else I know. This is probably a result of the fact that he has a strange tendency to describe any eligible female between the ages of 16 and 30 as a cousin. The habit seems to have started a few years ago when Oily, who was engaged at the time, was spotted by his fiancée coming out of a restaurant with an extremely curvaceous blonde clinging to his arm as if he were a wall and she were a particularly affectionate ivy. When confronted by his intended the following day Oily explained that the young lady was a long lost cousin. Since then he has discovered new cousins fairly regularly. Most, to no one's surprise, have been blonde, all of them have been shapely and none of them have been shy.

Oily said that the cousin who wanted to learn how to play golf had never seen a course or a ball before but had asked for a lesson on a whim. Always a gentleman and keen to oblige Oily had arranged a suitable date and fixed to meet his pupil on the first tee.

He had, however, omitted to tell her what to wear and on the appointed day she turned up wearing an extremely short, white tennis skirt and a flimsy, diaphanous tennis blouse. Such clothes can undoubtedly be distracting enough when they are worn by a player on the other side of a tennis net. When worn by a luscious young woman who needs to be shown how to hold a golf club they can, Oily assured me, produce disastrous consequences.

Oily said that when he put his arms around her to guide her hands onto the shaft of a three wood he could feel the sweat breaking out on his forehead and his body responding to her inspiration in all the other usual ways. He said he couldn't cope with giving her much of a lesson and simply told her to get on with it.

The next few holes were, he insisted, the most extraordinary holes of golf he'd ever played. He said that he still goes hot and cold inside when he thinks of them. The first couple of shots were apparently managed without much of a gallery but by the time they had reached the second green Oily insists that there were at least a dozen members within ten yards. A couple were standing around offering practical advice, one or two were pretending to talk to Oily and half a dozen seemed to be looking for lost balls. Three of the younger groundsmen started following them around raking out every bunker as Oily and his cousin approached it.

Oily said that every time his cousin took a big swing at the ball her skirt swirled up around her waist and her blouse strained at the seams. He said that she was a well built young girl. He said it got even worse when she started crouching over her putter. He said the other members didn't know whether to stand behind her or in front of her.

'I've never known so many members of the golf club keen to offer advice and help,' Oily insisted. He said that when they got to the third green there was a small queue of players wanting to offer practical help and that it took them all thirty minutes to decide just how the ball was likely to run on the green.

Oily said that by the time they had reached the fourth tee his cousin had decided that golf was obviously great fun. He said she honestly seemed to think it was a team game.

'There were at least three foursomes behind us,' said Oily. 'But none of them wanted to play through. They all said they were quite prepared to wait and perfectly willing to offer any help that might be necessary.'

Oily said that one or two of the spectators they'd acquired were quite overcome with emotion when his cousin took her first swing at the ball on the sixth tee. An elderly member, a former bank manager, collapsed in all the excitement and had to be wheeled back to the clubhouse on his trolley. There was, said Oily, a nasty moment when it looked as though no one was going to be prepared to go back to the clubhouse with the unfortunate fellow.

The lesson had to be abandoned on the ninth tee. Apparently his cousin's blouse, unable to cope with the strain, lost three buttons at a single stroke. Oily said that his cousin would have been happy to go on playing, insisting that she was just beginning to enjoy herself, but that the police inspector who had by now appeared to help control the crowds had advised him that it might be best if they abandoned the game for the day before any serious damage was done. Oily said he'd heard later that the casualty department at the local hospital had rung through to find out why so many elderly men in golfing attire were being wheeled in suffering from weakness and emotional exhaustion.

By the time Oily had finished telling his story (I sometimes suspect that he exaggerates a little but I know from personal experience that there is far more than a grain of truth in his reminiscences) Sharon had been at the wicket for several minutes, had scored two runs and had restored the team's good fortune.

She was lucky not to be out the first ball she received. The ball, a very slow full toss, hit the edge of her bat and bounced straight into the hands of forward short leg. He juggled with it for a moment before putting it down.

She had another lucky escape two balls later. This time the ball ricochetted off her bat and bounced fairly harmlessly past point. At the other end June, who was backing up enthusiastically shouted 'yes' and started to run. The fielder only had to cover two or three yards to fetch the ball but he seemed mesmerised and even when he had the ball in his hand he seemed unwilling to part with it. Eventually, by the time the ball had found its way via the wicket keeper to the bowler's end, Sharon had managed to sway her way down the pitch safely.

I don't know whether it was the fact that Sharon's presence on the pitch simply had such an effect on the Combe Regis players that they couldn't play properly, or whether they were reluctant to see the innings end and her disappear from the crease but she and June managed to bat on for twenty five minutes and score a valuable 22 runs before June was bowled trying to hit a half volley for six.

We were all out for 94. We knew it wasn't enough but at least our defeat would look dignified.

*   *   *

CHAPTER EIGHT

During the tea interval the Combe Regis captain came over to talk to Wodger.

'Congratulations on a fine performance,' he said. He smiled condescendingly. 'Of course, as you discovered, we have some very fine bowlers.' He stroked the area where a chin would have been if he'd had one. 'You had some uncommon good luck, though, I'm sure you'll agree.'

Wodger tried to look pleased, humble, embarrassed and slightly disbelieving and ended up looking rather simple minded.

'With regard to your accommodation this evening,' continued the Combe Regis captain. Slowly the rest of us gathered round, not because we were interested in what he had to say but because we'd never heard anyone talk like that before. He sounded like a circular from a civil servant. We listened politely. 'We'll look after you according to the batting order,' he went on. 'You number one batsman will stay with our number one batsman, your number two batsman will stay with our number two batsman and so on.' He looked around to make sure that we understood this and raised a questioning eyebrow. 'Is that acceptable?'

No one spoke. But it wasn't difficult to see that the plan was not widely received with enthusiasm. Sharon was looking at Oily and feverishly shaking her head. The vicar and June were both trying hard not to look disappointed.

'We'll give you the precise details at the end of the match,' added the Combe Regis captain, clearly keen not to burden us with too much information.

And with that he nodded to Wodger, gave us all a chance

to enjoy one of his smiles, turned sharply on his heel and left.

I looked around. Simon looked close to tears. Jerry looked glum. Only Arthur failed to show any emotion. He was lying semi-conscious a few yards away.

No one spoke for a minute or more. It was Brian who broke the silence.

'Do we have to stay with them?' he asked. 'A pub would be much more fun.' He looked around for support. The rest of us nodded and murmured our agreement.

Wodger looked distinctly uncomfortable. 'It would be very impolite not to accept their offer,' he told us sternly. 'Its very kind of them,' he added, unconvincingly.

We sprawled on the grass, sipping cups of tea and munching thinly sliced cucumber sandwiches prepared by three of the Combe Regis wives. The sandwiches had the crusts cut off the bread and even the cucumber had been skinned before being sliced wafer thin.

I turned to Oily to ask him if he could think of any way of getting out of our social obligation to the Combe Regis team. But he'd disappeared.

I looked around and eventually spotted him deep in conversation with the umpire who'd helped us reach our semi-respectable score. The umpire seemed to be complaining about something and Oily seemed to be commiserating with him. Oily isn't the sort of fellow who readily offers sympathy to strangers and I found his behaviour slightly puzzling.

'Have you heard from your old man, yet?' Brian asked June Tate.

June turned to him and blushed. She shook her head. 'Not a word,' she said. 'He knows where we are,' she pointed out. The vicar, sitting next to her, reached across and patted her hand in a clerical sort of way. She turned and smiled at him.

'Funny that,' said Brian to no one in particular. 'Him just disappearing.'

'I don't think he approved of me coming along,' said June. 'He's a bit funny about things sometimes.'

We all know that Sergeant Tate is a bit funny about things sometimes so we all nodded sagely.

'You've all been very kind to me,' said June.

Jerry mumbled something inaudible and the vicar put a kindly arm around her shoulders. June leant in towards him and put a grateful hand on his knee.

'We'd better wake Arthur up,' said Oily suddenly. I hadn't noticed him come back across to where we were sitting. 'The umpires are getting ready to go out.'

Wodger sent Simon into the dressing room to find Arthur's pads while he and Jerry tried to wake our wicket keeper by gently slapping his face.

'Is he all right?' asked the Combe Regis captain who'd wandered over again. He was padded up ready to bat. He wore a forearm shield and carried a brand new visored helmet and a thigh pad bulged under his immaculate flannels. He had an orange and vermillion silk scarf knotted around his neck.

'Its OK,' said Brian. 'He's only drunk.'

The Combe Regis captain involuntarily stepped back a pace as though afraid that, despite his armour, he might be contaminated by Arthur's condition.

'Its OK,' Oily reassured him. 'Its not infectious.'

The Combe Regis captain looked at Oily with distaste. 'I know that,' he snapped. 'My wife is a doctor.'

'Looking forward to your innings?' Oily asked, with a sneer in his voice. Oily share his disrespect generously.

'I think we might be able to show you a thing or two,' smiled the Combe Regis captain, patronisingly.

'Fancy your chances, then?' Oily asked him.

The Combe Regis captain looked startled; as though it had never even occurred to him that his team's success might be in any question, let alone that it might depend on anything as unpredictable as 'chance'.

'Don't suppose you feel confident enough for a bit of a wager?' said Oily. He dragged the word 'wager' out and grinned impudently.

The Combe Regis captain scowled. 'A bet?' he said. He paused and looked at Oily. 'You're prepared to bet on *your* side winning?' he asked incredulously. He put a scornful amount of emphasis on the word 'your'.

'Of course,' said Oily. 'I wouldn't bet on you lot.' He turned and looked at Arthur. 'How's he doing?' he asked.

'He'll be all right,' replied Brian. He and Jerry had woken

65

Arthur up and were trying to persuade him to see if he could stand. To be honest Arthur looked fairly fit.

'I couldn't take your money from you,' said the Combe Regis captain, his lip curling as he stared in disgust at our merry wicket keeper. Arthur hiccuped loudly.

'Give me decent odds then,' Oily suggested.

The captain of the home side thought for a moment. 'Ten to one,' he offered. 'I'll take your money at ten to one.'

'OK!' said Oily. 'Done.' He reached into his back pocket and pulled out a wafer thin Alligator skin wallet. The Combe Regis captain looked at the thickness of the wallet and sniffed. Oily opened the wallet, took out five £50 notes and spread them out so that the Combe Regis captain could see them clearly. 'Who's going to hold the stake?' he asked.

I thought the Combe Regis captain paled a fraction at the size of the bet. He and the rest of us realised at the same moment that he stood to lose £2500 on the match.

Oily, still holding the five bank notes repeated his question.

'There's no need for that,' said the Combe Regis captain. 'I assume we're all gentlemen here.' With that he scowled at Oily, turned away and marched back to join his team.

'Bloody hell,' said Jerry. 'Thats some bet!'

Wodger looked distinctly uncomfortable. 'If we win I won't like taking advantage of their hospitality,' he said, shaking his head.

'If we win we won't be taking advantage of anyone's hospitality,' said Oily with a broad grin. 'Two and a half grand will pay for rooms in the best hotel we can find.'

I think it was that prospect which wound us all up more than the worry of seeing Oily lose £250. We all knew he could afford that easily. But none of us found the idea of splitting up and spending the night with total strangers particularly attractive.

'Do you think we can do it?' asked Simon, breathlessly. He was flushed with excitement.

'Of course we can,' Oily assured him. 'Its in the bag.' He winked at Simon. 'You wanna bet too?'

'Oh, no!' said Simon quickly. 'No, thank you!'

*　　*　　*

Cricketers – and spectators – have always liked betting on cricket matches. The two have a long and close relationship. Back in the 19th century thousands of pounds would be bet on a single day's cricket and fortunes could be made or lost on the result of an afternoon's game.

Personally, I don't believe in betting any more. I only gambled the once but I lost so convincingly that it cured me of the temptation for life.

It was at a county match a few years ago. To be precise it was a match held at the beautiful ground in Worcester. The home side were playing Nottinghamshire and I'd gone to watch the match – a one day Sunday fixture – with an acquaintance I'd met through business. I didn't know him particularly well but he had tickets for the match since his firm was one of the sponsors.

'Do you fancy a bet?' he asked me as we settled ourselves down near to his firm's hospitality tent. They'd hired a bevy of attractive young girls to serve us wine, beer and sandwiches and I honestly thought I must have died and gone to heaven without noticing anything.

I muttered something about not being much of a betting man. The truth was that unless you count the occasional flutter in the works Grand National sweepstake I'd never bet before in my life.

My acquaintance ignored me. 'I bet you that I can forecast the score of every batsman on both sides within 3 runs.'

I looked at him as though he'd gone stark raving mad.

'Really!' he insisted. 'I'm dead good at this.'

'Oh, no, I couldn't.' I protested.

'Every batsman's score to within three runs,' he said. 'I'll get a spare scorecard and write in all my predictions. We'll then give the scorecard to someone to keep.' He looked around and mentioned the name of someone he knew that we both trusted. 'At the end of the match we'll compare the official scorecard and my scorecard and see what I got right.'

'But thats impossible!' I insisted, realising that each batsman could score anything from 0 to 200.

'So give me odds that mean I stand a chance,' he said. He thought for a moment. 'Ten to one,' he suggested.

I shook my head. 'Oh, no!' I said. 'I couldn't.'

'Twenty to one then?'

I thought for a moment. I really didn't like taking his money off him. The odds against him winning seemed outrageous. But the bet was becoming irresistible. And he was so keen that it seemed almost churlish to refuse.

'Pound a player,' he suggested. 'You get £1 for every player whose score isn't within 3 runs of my prediction. And I get £20 for every player I get within 3 runs.'

I thought again. I guessed he might hit lucky and get one right. That would mean that at worst I'd end up even. And if he got them all wrong I could always refuse to take his money off him.

'OK!' I said, still reluctantly.

'Fine,' said my acquaintance. 'I'll go and write out my predictions.' He got up and disappeared for a couple of minutes.

'Tom's got the scorecard,' he said, when he returned. I looked round and Tom waved a scorecard, carefully folded it and put it away in his inside jacket pocket. He winked at me conspiratorially.

I still felt bad about the bet but the game was good, the waitresses pretty and the booze plentiful. Within half an hour I'd put it to the back of my mind and by tea time I'd forgotten about the bet completely.

At the end of the match – Worcester had won by a whisker – my acquaintance jumped up.

'Right!' he said, rubbing his hands. 'Time to check on my scorecard!'

I must have looked puzzled.

'Our bet!' he reminded me.

'Oh, don't worry about that,' I insisted magnanimously.

'Have to,' he insisted. 'Its a bet.'

He stood up and made his way through the disappearing crowd. A couple of minutes later he reappeared with Tom in tow.

'The card please . . .!' said my acquaintance to our Trustee.

Tom reached into his pocket, took out the folded scorecard and handed it to me.

'Here's a card of the final scores,' said my acquaintance, producing a neatly filled in scorecard. 'Lets check them out.'

I still felt bad about it. I was worried about how much

I was going to win. I opened the card that my acquaintance had completed before the match and looked down the two sides. To my surprise he had predicted exactly the same score for each player. by the side of each name was clearly written a figure '3'.

I suddenly felt cold inside – and very sober.

Together we worked our way down the official scorecard, comparing each player's score with the pre-match prediction.

Altogether fifteen players had batted. Six out of the fifteen had scored within three runs of his prediction. This meant that I lost £120 and won £9.

As I wrote out a cheque for £111 I ruefully swore never to try betting again. If you look through a few old copies of Wisden you'll soon find the match concerned. I checked out a dozen other matches and discovered that at nearly all of them I would have lost heavily.

I remembered that miserable day as we trooped out onto the field behind the two umpires. I really couldn't see how we stood a chance of helping Oily win his bet – much as I wanted us to be able to do so.

* * *

CHAPTER NINE

The Combe Regis innings opened in a fairly spectacular fashion. So keen was the vicar to help Oily win his bet (his enthusiasm may have been enhanced by the knowledge that if we won we would probably be choosing our own sleeping arrangements in a local hotel rather than being split up and spending the night with the home team) that his first over contained three no balls and two wides. Even when the vicar managed to get his feet and the ball in the right spot the Combe Regis captain still treated his bowling with disdain. By the end of that first over they had scored 24 runs without the loss of a wicket.

Things looked up at the start of the second over when Jerry took over – though to be honest I'm not sure how much this was due to Jerry's bowling and how much it was due to the fact that the umpire at that end was the tiny fellow whose decisions had helped our batsman reach a relatively respectable score.

Jerry's third ball was slightly over pitched and it looked to me to be well outside the line of the off stump. The batsman, a huge, red faced fellow, took his eye off the ball, stepped down the wicket and swung his bat as though determined to send the ball into orbit. Unfortunately for him he missed completely and the ball hit his front pad square on.

For a moment I didn't think Jerry was even going to bother appealing. When he did it wasn't so much an appeal as an indication of desperation. It was the sort of appeal a bowler makes and regrets a split second later; the cricketing equivalent of a grown up putting a note up the chimney for Father Christmas.

The umpire didn't hesitate. His finger went up as though string operated.

For a moment no one seemed to notice. After his appeal Jerry automatically shook his head and started to walk back up the wicket, accepting the rejection that hadn't come. The batsman hadn't even bothered to look up at the umpire when he'd heard Jerry's appeal.

When everyone realised that the appeal *had* been successful the response was predictable confusion. Jerry hesitated for a moment and then leapt into the air in celebration. I'd never seen Jerry do that before. It wasn't the sort of thing he did. The batsman, opened mouthed and aghast, strode down the wicket to remonstrate with the umpire. The Combe Regis captain, torn between a feeling that he should respect the umpire's decision, support for his fellow opening batsman, dismay at the loss of a valuable wicket, and genuine surprise, didn't seem sure what to do. Eventually he simply prodded the wicket angrily with his bat and glowered at Wodger who had rushed over to congratulate Jerry.

Two overs later it happened again. This time Jerry sent down a ball that started on the leg side and seemed destined to test Arthur's agility more than usual. Somehow the batsman, the youngest player in the Combe Regis side, managed to move across far enough to flick the ball with his pad after missing it completely with the bat. From where I was standing it looked more like a wide than anything else. But the umpire didn't hesitate when he heard Jerry's appeal.

Suddenly, from being 24 for 0 the Combe Regis side had slumped to 28 for 2.

Three balls later I took the best catch of my life to dismiss the next batsman.

Jerry, brimming with confidence now, was bowling faster than any of us had ever seen him bowl before. He produced a ball that any professional would have been proud of. That's one of the magnificent things about cricket. Just occasionally even the worst batsman in the world will produce a stroke of world class authority and every once in a while a very ordinary bowler (not that I'm suggesting for an instant that Jerry's bowling could normally be described as 'ordinary') will produce a ball that has 'class' written all over it from the moment it leaves his hand.

The batsman played straight down the line intending to lift the ball straight back over Jerry's head. He got an edge and the ball soared higher and higher until I could hardly see it at all. For a while I watched it dispassionately, an innocent spectator bemused by this apparent denial of gravity. It looked as though the ball was never going to come down again.

And then I realised that from the position my neck was in it was beginning to look as though the responsibility for taking the catch would be mine.

It would be an understatement to say that I was horrified. The responsibility appalled me. The consequences terrified me. I looked around quickly to see if any one else was around and, to my total delight, saw that Norman, who'd been fielding near me at deep square-leg was running across to where I was standing.

'Mine!' shouted Norman, with uncharacteristic certainty.

I stepped back out of the way and watched him run forwards, his eyes fixed on the ball as it hung, apparently suspended, in space.

'Yours!' he said suddenly, with equal certainty.

Panicking, I moved forwards a few feet and looked up. I couldn't tell whether the ball was still going up or had started coming down. It seemed to be hovering right over me.

'Mine!' shouted Norman suddenly. He was standing right beside me.

I tried to move away again.

'Yours!' he cried almost immediately.

I snapped my head back and looked up. This time there was no mistake about it. The ball had finished toying with Isaac Newton's laws and was now quite definitely earthbound. It was hurtling down towards me at the speed of a bullet.

'Catch it!' shouted some distant fool.

I fixed my eyes on the ball and put my hands together as though in prayer. I cupped them slightly, held them to my chest and began to pray.

The ball thudded into my hands and I grasped it as though my life depended on it. My fingers and palms tingled with pain and the shock of the ball's landing pushed me down to my knees but I caught it.

I never know what to do when I've taken a catch. Maybe more practice would help solve this dilemma but I am always slightly embarrassed and bewildered. Should I simply toss the ball to the wicket keeper and modestly reassume my position in the field? Should I stand there and wait for my fellow fielders to gather round and offer their congratulations? Should I expect kisses? Applause? Plaudits of approbation? Should I throw the ball straight back into the sky as the professionals sometimes do? And if I do should I try to catch it again – to prove that the catch was no fluke – or should I simply let it fly off into the unknown? Should I rush over with the ball and congratulate the bowler? Should I offer sympathy to the batsman?

I simply stood there glowing with pride and feeling relief flowing through my body like a comforting heat.

Combe Regis were now 28 for 3 and their captain, still at the wicket, was beginning to look uncomfortable.

It was twenty minutes before we took another wicket and by then the home side had managed to take their score to 40.

This time the victorious bowler was Brian, bowling, almost inevitably perhaps, at the end where Jerry had had his earlier successes. All the bowlers were desperate to bowl at that end; no one was unaware that the umpire there was far more sympathetic to our cause than his colleague.

But Brian's first wicket owed nothing at all to the umpire. The ball with which he dismissed the Combe Regis captain was slow, well pitched up and didn't turn at all. But somehow the remaining Combe Regis opener missed it entirely. The ball slipped straight past his prodding bat, past his pads and onto the stumps. It wasn't travelling fast enough to knock the stumps out of the ground and simply fell, as though stunned, at the base of the wicket. The two bails landed on top of it and remained exactly where they'd fallen.

We all cheered Brian's success. Both June and Sharon rushed over and kissed him full on the mouth, and although we usually frown on that sort of thing in our side Brian didn't seem to mind at all.

At 40 for 4 the match was evenly balanced and our total

of 94 no longer looked as vulnerable as it had when we'd completed our innings. The last wicket stand between Sharon and June was beginning to look all the more valuable.

Just when we were beginning to feel more confident, however, the Combe Regis side managed to rebuild their own shattering hopes. Slowly, our bowling began to look ragged and unthreatening. The two batsmen at the crease began to dominate the slow bowling partnership of Brian and Simon, and Wodger had to bring the vicar and Jerry back into the attack. After another forty minutes the score, from a promising 40 for 4, had become a distinctly dangerous 68 for 4. They only needed another 27 runs to win.

Jerry and the vicar had changed ends (there would have been bloodshed if they hadn't) and it was, perhaps not surprisingly, the vicar who broke through and kept our vanishing hopes alive. Once again it was an lbw decision and once again I think we were lucky. The batsman looked furious as he reluctantly left the crease and the vicar looked guilty rather than proud.

That made it 68 for 5. It was anyone's match.

It was then that Wodger showed why he is, and deserves to be, our captain. He displayed wisdom, aggression and leadership in a single, bold move. He brought Sharon in from the deep to field at silly mid-off.

In previous matches June had caused some confusion among our opponents by her presence. She is an attractive and shapely woman. But June would not dream of flaunting her sexuality. Though generous and warm hearted she guards her charms and preserves her passion for the few rather than the many.

Sharon, it was already clear, had none of June's reservations. She clearly enjoyed making her presence felt among members of the opposite sex. And she was not hampered by self consciousness or unnatural modesty.

I don't think it's necessary to explain Sharon's tactics in close detail. I think it is probably enough to explain that when Sharon fielded close the Combe Regis batsmen found it difficult to keep their attention on the ball.

Almost before they knew what was happening to them two had been clean bowled and one caught behind by Arthur.

Sharon's name did not appear in the scorebook but it should have done. With those three wickets Sharon secured her place in our side for the rest of the tour as effectively as if she had scored a double century.

Combe Regis had slumped to 75 for 8.

The departing batsmen complained, of course. They argued that they had been unfairly distracted. They claimed that we were cheating. But the umpire instantly rejected their complaints as sexist and irrelevant.

We would, I think, have won easily if the remaining batsmen had shared their predecessors tastes. But, unfortunately, Sharon's charms lost their match winning quality with the arrival at the crease of the Combe Regis wicket keeper. We should have realised that he would be immune to Sharon's special skills when we saw him walking out to bat. But it was only when we saw him running between the wickets that we realised precisely why he seemed unaffected by our potential match winner.

The Combe Regis wicket keeper, like his partner, did not run so much as mince. Sharon's presence had about as much effect on him as it would have done on the average male window dresser. Indeed, just one over later Wodger had to remove Sharon from her potentially dangerous position and put her back in the relatively safety of the outfield. The Combe Regis wicket keeper soon looked as though he was going to turn the match single handed.

As the Combe Regis total moved slowly but inexorably through the eighties we began to lose hope. Our total just wasn't enough.

But then our luck turned again.

With the Combe Regis score on 92 for 8 it looked as though we were beaten. They needed just three runs for victory. We needed two wickets.

The vicar got the wickets we needed with consecutive balls. Both batsmen were out lbw.

We had won.

*   *   *

The Combe Regis players were determined not to show their disappointment or frustration. They congratulated us with thin lipped smiles and limp, brief handshakes and tried to look convinced when Wodger condescendingly offered them his condolences and reminded them that cricket is only a game.

Their captain, who had rushed into the home side dressing room at the end of the match, was white when he reappeared a few minutes later. He'd slipped his blazer over his cricket gear and the brightly coloured scarf that he still wore around his neck contrasted vividly with his pallor.

'I'm afraid it will have to be a cheque,' he said to Oily through clenched teeth. 'I don't have that much cash on me.'

'No problem!' Oily assured him. 'Just make it out to cash, will you? I'll take it along to the bank in the morning if thats OK with you.'

'Two thousand five hundred pounds?' said the captain as though hoping that Oily would correct him.

'That's right!' Oily nodded cheerfully. I almost felt embarrassed as I watched the Combe Regis captain struggling to keep his hand steady as he wrote out the cheque. But then I remembered how patronising he'd been and I managed to suppress the feeling.

'Er ...' said Wodger, who'd been standing nearly, 'about the ... er ... accomodation ...'. He looked distinctly uncomfortable.

The Combe Regis captain tore the completed cheque out of his cheque book and handed it over to Oily who read it carefully, folded it and stuffed it into his trouser pocket.

'It was very good of you to offer ...' Wodger carried on, 'but on reflection we've got a long journey ...' he paused again and looked around for help. No one else said anything. 'Maybe we ought to move on down the coast tonight ...' he concluded tamely.

The Combe Regis captain put his cheque book away in his inside jacket pocket and shrugged slightly. 'Whatever you think best,' he said. Then he turned away, stared briefly as Arthur who had collapsed again and was now lying unconscious on the grass, and walked back to his dressing room.

We didn't wait to shower or change. We simply threw our bats, pads, gloves, bags and clothes into the three cars and left. Wodger had an RAC book and said he'd lead us to the

76

nearest pub. Oily repeated his promise to buy us all accommodation in the best local hotel we could find and instructed Wodger that we wouldn't settle for anything that didn't have more stars than the Milky Way.

I tried to resist the temptation to ask Oily the question that I knew I didn't really want answered but in the end I could contain my curiosity no longer.

'How did you know that we were going to win?' I asked him, as we followed Wodger's cautious progress through the narrow Devon lanes leading away from Combe Regis.

'What do you mean?' asked Oily, in mock indignation. 'It was a bet.'

'I know you,' I reminded him. 'You only bet if you've got an edge. What was your edge?'

For a minute or so Oily didn't speak. He was enjoying his little secret.

'I had a chat with one of their umpires,' Oily said. 'During the tea interval.'

'I saw you.'

'He hates the Combe Regis captain,' said Oily with a broad grin.

'Why?'

'The Combe Regis captain has been having an affair with his wife,' Oily told me. 'The poor little chap only found out yesterday.'

'And I don't suppose the captain knows that he knows yet?'

'He may have worked it out by now.'

Slowly it all fell into place.

'So all these dodgy lbw decisions were his way of getting his own back?'

'I like to think I helped give his revenge a little extra spice,' said Oily. 'I told him I was going to have a bet on the outcome of the match.'

'It's a lot of money,' I said. 'Can he afford it?'

'He's a solicitor,' said Oily. 'Who cares whether or not he can afford it?'

*   *   *

CHAPTER TEN

I was woken by the sound of a bell. For a moment I couldn't work out where the noise was coming from. But as I slowly dragged myself back into the land of the living I gradually realised where I was. I reached across to my left and picked up the telephone. The ringing stopped immediately.

'Your morning call, sir!' chirped a hideously cheerful receptionist at the other end of the line.

'What?' I demanded. I've never asked for a morning call in my life. I've always worked on the simple basis that God will get me up when he wants me to be up and about.

'Its seven o'clock!' the receptionist informed me as though expecting me to receive this news with glee.

I put the phone down. 'Thank you!' I said too late.

Wearily, I rubbed my fingers through my hair and scratched my scalp. I had, I reckoned, had about five minutes sleep all night. And I knew it was pointless trying to get any more. I wondered who'd ordered the early morning call.

I switched on my bedside light and with the aid of its shadowy 40 watts peered around the room. Arthur was lying flat on his back making a noise like a distressed elephant in labour. I read somewhere that when he snores an ordinary man can make as much noise as a pneumatic drill. No one could possibly describe Arthur as an ordinary man and the sound he makes when he snores is no ordinary sound. A dozen turbo charged pneumatic drills would have been as butterflies fluttering in a vacuum compared to the noise Arthur was making.

Lying curled up on a makeshift child's bed, that two surly porters had squeezed into position across the ends of our two beds, Simon seemed oblivious to it all. It was a long time since I'd seen such a vision of innocence. He had the tip of his right thumb in his mouth and his pyjamas, I noticed, were covered with tiny pink lambs.

When we'd left Combe Regis we'd driven down to Newquay, the biggest resort on the northern coast and the venue for our next cricket match. Encouraged by Oily and aided by his four year old RAC guidebook Wodger had taken us to The Royal Grand Atlantic hotel, an impressive, grey Victorian building which was decorated with several illuminated signs confirming its status and desirability.

The hotel was situated right on the promenade with spectacular views of the sea and foreshore and it seemed ideal. The only snag was that the receptionist, an astonishingly elegant young woman who had clearly spent much of her life polishing and painting her nails, was only able to offer us five rooms.

Oily and Sharon offered to share one as, with expected generosity, did June and the vicar. Wodger, as captain, announced that he would take the only single room. That meant that Jerry, Brian, Norman, Arthur, Simon and I would have to share the remaining two rooms.

I've never liked sharing rooms with men – especially cricketers. A few years ago I went on a tour of East Anglia with a team from my old school. I can't remember whether it was through an earnest sense of economy or a misguided determination to meld us together into a team but the captain, a psychology student at a Scottish University, had arranged for us all to share rooms. He explained his occupation of a single room by reminding us of his extra responsibilities.

I found myself sharing a room with one of the most neurotic human beings I have ever met. His name was Peter and I still come out in a rash when I think of him.

It's a few years since the tour took place and my subconscious has, at last, managed to suppress most of the memories which seemed at the time to be carving permanent spots for themselves – but I can still remember our first night together.

We went to our room early; bathed, cleaned our teeth and got into our twin beds. I was looking forward to reading a few pages of a thriller I was enjoying.

'I don't think I'll be able to sleep,' said Peter suddenly.

I looked up from my book.

'The match tomorrow,' Peter explained.

I waited.

'I always get nervous before a match.'

I made some sort of sympathetic noise and looked down at my book again.

'It's the responsibility that really gets to me,' said Peter.

I found my bookmark and closed my book. I should at this point perhaps explain that Peter was probably the worst cricketer ever to hold a bat or ball. He never bowled, couldn't bat and had to be hidden somewhere in the outfield where he was unlikely to get in anyone else's way. He got his place in the team because he worked for a coach company and could rent their most luxurious model for next to nothing.

'People don't realise,' said Peter, glumly.

I turned off my bedside light in the hope that Peter would get the message.

'Batting at number eleven is a tremendous responsibility,' insisted Peter. He was still sitting upright in bed, his hands clasped neatly and his copy of Stamp Collectors Monthly arranged precisely but unopened in front of him.

'Goodnight, Peter!' I said, hopefully.

'It's the most difficult place in the batting order,' Peter went on. 'People who haven't batted there don't realise.'

I grunted.

'The chap who bats at number ten is OK. There's always someone coming after him. But if you bat at number eleven there's no one else to take the responsibility off your shoulders.'

I opened an eye. Peter hadn't moved. His bedside lamp was still switched on and he sat bathed in its gentle light.

'Whatever happen there's a terrible responsibility.' Peter looked across at me. I quickly closed my eye. 'The chap at the other end is probably close to his 50 or his 100,' said Peter. 'The team may need another half a dozen runs to win the match.'

'You can only make one mistake as a batsman,' said Peter. I resisted the temptation to point out to him that he has probably made as many mistakes as he has faced balls. 'Batting at number eleven puts a terrible burden on a fellow.'

It went on like this for hours.

I lay there for a while but eventually I could see that I wasn't going to get any sleep so I gave up, turned my light on and opened my book again.

Two hours later he stopped talking.

I looked across. He'd fallen asleep in mid sentence. He was luckier than I was. Four hours later I was still awake. I'd finished my book and his stamp magazine and ended up reading the bible I'd found in the drawer of my bedside cabinet.

Neither Arthur nor Simon could be described as neurotic but they had both conspired successfully to keep my awake. Arthur through his snoring and Simon through giggling at Arthur. Arthur had been asleep when we'd put him into his bed (or maybe unconscious would have been a more accurate description) and even Simon had managed to fall asleep eventually. But for me it had been a long, noisy and disturbed night.

If there's one thing that annoys me more than lying in bed unable to get to sleep it's lying in bed unable to get to sleep and watching other people sleep. I jumped out of bed, drew the curtains and gently shook Simon by the shoulder.

'Time to get up!' I told him. 'It's a glorious day!'

It was too. The sun was already up and the day promised much. The view from our room was truly spectacular. Newquay is a well developed resort but it still has the raw wild charm of that northern coastline. There was hardly any breeze but the sea was crashing rhythmically on the distant rocks.

Simon didn't need waking twice. He threw his bedclothes to one side, jumped out of bed and rushed over to the window.

'What a view!' he said, full of excitement. 'Isn't this tour wonderful? I wish it could go on for ever. Did they ring to wake us up? The porter downstairs asked if we wanted an early morning call and I've never had a morning call before so I said 'yes'. Shall we go and wake the others? Where do you think we have breakfast?'

His enthusiasm pulled me from the brink of gloom. When Arthur suddenly grunted, rolled over and fell out of bed I laughed.

Arthur didn't stop snoring even then. We lifted him back

81

into bed, then washed, shaved, and dressed ourselves and went down to breakfast.

* * *

After breakfast all of us except Arthur walked across the road in front of the hotel, down the steps and onto the beach. Arthur had woken briefly when Simon and I had returned to our room to clean our teeth and pack our clothes after breakfast but after taking a couple of long swigs from his never empty flask he had waved a cheery hand at us and pulled the bedclothes back over his head again.

Outside the sun was moving from warm to hot and the sand beneath our feet was already heating up. All of us except Wodger and the vicar had brought bathing trunks with us and we stripped off and changed in a small, shady area protected by rocks. Actually, to be precise, not all of us who changed had brought the proper swimming apparel with us. June had a very tasteful one piece bathing suit with her but Sharon simply took off her mini dress and allowed her matching white panties and bra to serve as an impromptu bikini.

After we had splashed around in the sea for a few minutes Jerry spotted a game of beach cricket being played by a group of teenage boys. While Wodger and the vicar stumbled after us with our clothes in their arms we raced one another across the beach towards them.

Five minutes later Wodger had lost the toss and was busily directing us to our fielding places. In Arthur's absence I found myself honoured with the position of acting wicket-keeper. I've always had a fondness for wicket keeping. You get a little sword by the side of your name on the score sheet but you don't have the awesome responsibilities of being captain. Since Wodger and the vicar were the only two of us who were still fully dressed they fielded furthest from the sea. The vicar got into the spirit of things by removing his shoes and socks and rolling up his trouser legs but Wodger, conscious of his responsibility and status, kept his shoes and socks on and allowed his grey flannels to flap unfettered.

I hadn't played beach cricket for over twenty years and most of our team seemed equally unemcumbered by experience. Jerry opened the bowling and quickly discovered that bowling with a balding tennis ball on firm sand requires an unusual type of skill. His first ball bounced way over the batsman's head, over my head and was stopped by Simon only after it had bounced off a large wooden noticeboard which warned holidaymakers DO NOT THROW STONES AT THIS NOTICE. His second ball hit a footprint on the pitch and bounced off in the direction of mid-wicket long before the batsman had a chance to get anywhere near to it.

Apart from Simon our other bowlers suffered equal discomfort and embarrassment. Simon was the only one of us young enough to remember the very special skills that beach cricket requires. He knew that even a modest spinner can make a tennis ball turn at right angles on damp sand and he therefore bowled with commendable caution and restraint, relying on line and length rather than anything spectacular.

The opposition batsman, not one of whom was old enough to take shaving seriously, regarded our bowling with some amusement. Defence shots play no part in beach cricket and they seemed to get enormous pleasure out of thrashing out at every ball with wild, baseball type swings, comfortable in the knowledge that even if they missed the ball would be extremely unlikely to hit their wicket. There is also something deeply comforting and reassuring about the fact that the ball is soft and unlikely to cause any lasting damage even if it hits an unusually vulnerable part of the human body.

But despite the enthusiasm of the batsmen it was the extras which accumulated fastest. By the time their last batsman had run himself out our smooth cheeked opponents had reached three figures with ease. It was, we all knew, a formidable score.

Our innings had been under way for fifteen or twenty minutes before any of us realised that we were facing a problem that none of us had encountered before. The tide was coming in – and coming in fast.

'Let's move the wickets,' said Wodger, putting down his bat, turning round and pulling two stumps out of the sand. He hopped about as he did so in a vain attempt to keep his shoes dry.

There was a loud chorus of disapproval and dissent from the fielding side.

'You can't do that!' said their leader, a tall, skinny, freckled youth who wore red trunks and a dirty bandage on his left elbow.

'But the tide's coming in!' explained Wodger, unnecessarily. 'The pitch is getting wet.'

'Natural playing conditions!' exclaimed the red trunked youth. 'You can't suddenly move the wickets because you suddenly don't like the playing conditions!'

He seemed to have the support of all his fellow team members and I confess that I found that his argument did contain an uncomfortable amount of logic.

'But the tide wasn't coming in when you batted!' protested Wodger.

But Wodger had lost the argument and he knew it. There are few things more embarrassing than the sight of a grown man wanting to change the rules when he's losing a game of cricket to a group of children. Wodger should have known better than to start such a confrontation. Our opponents were, after all, so young and innocent that they had regarded Sharon's presence in our side with lightly disguised disapproval. Cricket, they all knew, was not a game for girls but if we didn't know it that was our problem.

Our innings was a disaster of quite heroic proportions. It is difficult to play graceful and effective shots when the ball splashes soggily in several inches of seaweed laden surf before being dragged seawards by the undertow. It is difficult to crack a ball through the covers when the splash the ball makes temporarily blinds you with spray. It is difficult to move your feet to the pitch of the ball – in an attempt to turn a short pitched delivery into a full toss -when the water is up past your ankles and you are aware that if the ball should land and float past you out of reach the wicket keeper will have the imaginary bails off long before you can even turn round let alone run back to safety.

We scored a total of 11 and 6 of those were extras.

*   *   *

CHAPTER ELEVEN

After our last wicket fell (it was the first time I'd ever seen eight stumpings and two run outs in one innings) Oily attempted to re-establish our status as cricketers of grace and generosity by buying our young opponents a round of large ice cream cornets each of which was decorated with a stick of flaky chocolate.

It was while Oily was settling the bill with the ice cream salesman (and struggling unsuccessfully to negotiate a bulk discount) that I noticed one of our erstwhile opponents sitting on a rock glumly examining the bat we'd all been using and allowing his untouched ice cream to drip messily into the sand. There was an unmistakeable tear coursing down his left cheek.

Equipment is never a crucial factor in beach cricket. I have seen people using a furled umbrella as a bat and having tremendous fun. But, in addition to the balding tennis ball our match had been played with a set of six professionally turned stumps and an ancient, heavy cricket bat which bore the fading stamped signature of Denis Compton and which had clearly been involved in its long life in many crucial and memorable cricket campaigns.

It's true that, after a lifetime of heavy use, the bat had acquired so many layers of bandage that hardly any of its original willow was visible but it was, nevertheless, a proper cricket bat and not an umbrella. It deserved to be taken seriously.

'What's up?' I asked the glum and cheerless child.

He slowly lifted his head and looked up at me. There was a deep and searing sadness in his young eyes.

'My bat's broken,' he said after a moment's hesitation.

I held my hand out for the bat and when, with reluctance, he eventually handed it to me, examined it. He was right. The splice between handle and blade was fractured and the bat seemed to have no future.

'Did we do this?' I asked him.

The boy looked up at me and then, almost imperceptibly lifted his shoulders in a pitiful expression of uncertainty.

'It seemed OK when we were playing,' I said.

'What's the matter?' asked Norman, who'd joined us.

I explained.

'That's a terrible shame!' said Norman, genuinely sympathetic.

'Let's go and get you a new one,' I said. 'Where's the nearest sports shop?'

* * *

Sports equipment shops are little more than toyshops in disguise.

I once used to play golf with a fellow who was quite convinced that one day he would find some piece of equipment which would revolutionise his game, prevent him ever topping a ball again and cure his long standing habit of slicing the ball. He used to spend a fortune in the professional's shop at the course where he played. He must have been one of golf's best customers. If he'd chosen to take up fishing instead of golf several major international companies would have probably been forced to seek alternative sources of finance. Instead of having huge factories on large industrial estates they would have probably been struggling along in converted garages in Balham.

Every time we came out of the locker rooms changed and ready to play he would decide that he'd just have to slip into the professional's shop for a moment. He went on the pretext that he needed to buy a tee, though his golf bag was stuffed with enough tees to carpet the average sized fairway. Once he got inside the shop he would behave just as a small boy would behave in a sweet shop. Wide eyed and full of perpetual innocence he would wander around looking at everything as though he'd never seen it before.

Then he would, apparently idly and without real interest, select a club from the rack. 'Is this new?' he'd ask the professional who would have been hovering nearby in anticipation of the request.

'It's just come in,' the professional would assure him in a conspiratorial whisper. 'I think its the only one I've got.' The professional would then saunter forward slowly and take the club from my friend with exaggerated care. He would fondle the shaft, the head and the grip and look as though he was about to sell a favourite daughter into slavery. I've seen antique dealers use exactly the same technique.

'It's absolutely revolutionary,' he would whisper. Then he would rub his fingers up and down the club and point out some special marking or some other modest peculiarity.

'Look at that!' He'd tell my friend. 'Have you ever seen anything like that before?'

My friend, already convinced and desperate to buy, would shake his head as though hypnotised.

'There's already talk that the Royal and Ancient might try to ban it because it will make the whole game too easy,' the professional would whisper, looking over his shoulder as though to make sure that no one else was listening. 'But for the moment it's perfectly legal ... there's nothing anyone can do to stop a player using one of these ... nothing in the rules as they stand.'

And that would be that. Having gone into the shop for a golf tee my friend would walk out with yet another armful of metalwork. He had more than enough clubs to equip both sides in the Ryder Cup.

Not that he limited himself to clubs, of course. Sometimes it would be a set of specially made soft leather golf club head covers. Occasionally it would be a new trolley with extra wide wheels and a spring loaded brake. Or it would be a dozen specially formulated uncuttable golf balls, all of which he would lose long before he hit them hard enough to test the manufacturer's promise.

He used to buy armfuls of gadgets and his friends and relatives were never at a loss to know what to buy him for Christmas or for his birthday. He had special suede non stick putting gloves; super absorbent towels for drying his hands, clubs and balls; a giant sized umbrella with an automatic closing button as well as a button for opening it; special golfing binoculars fitted with an electronic range finder; several different types of putting trainer; a driving range for his back lawn; special golf shoes with a swivel built into the sole of the left shoe and a herd of golf bags which filled his garage and kept his car out in the snow and rain in winter.

In the past choosing cricket equipment was never such a hazardous or potentially expensive hobby. You went into the sports shop when you decided to start playing cricket and bought yourself a bat, a pair of pads and a pair of gloves. You collected a pair of flannels, a white shirt, a sweater, a pair of good boots and a pair of white socks. You were reminded by the assistant that you'd need a box and if you had any money left you might have spent it on a bag into which you could cram all your gear.

Regularly, every ten years, you would return to the shop to buy another pair of white socks, another bottle of linseed oil and some more strapping for the bat. You would look at the prices of new bats with a mixture of astonishment and horror and you would give thanks that you'd bought your bat years before inflation hit the game.

It's not like that any more. Today's cricketer is as vulnerable to commercial exploitation as yesterday's golfer.

Today's cricketer can choose between several different types of helmet. There are thigh pads, elbow guards and chest protectors to be studied. There are ankle pads, a dozen varieties of batting glove and sun hats and visors to compete with the traditional batting cap.

In the old days choosing a bat was fairly simple. You'd pick up a couple of bats and play a few imaginary strokes with them. You'd execute half a dozen perfect cover drives and marvel at the ability of the salesman to remain unimpressed by your genius. You'd check to make sure that all the bats had handles stout enough for knocking in the stumps and then you'd choose the bat that had the best inscription and the most impressive signature at the top of the blade.

It's all changed. These days there are bats with bits cut out of the back and bats with bits hollowed out from the sides. There are bats with special coatings (linseed oil is as old fashioned as the leg break bowler) and bats with scientifically approved springing in the handles. Bats are designed by ergonometricians rather than signed by Test players. There are rows of them and they cost so much that you can probably get a mortgage if you ask for one.

The twenty four of us crowded into the sports shop (we'd discovered rather belatedly that our opponents side had 14 members) and twenty three of us watched and gave unheeded advice as the small boy with the broken bat selected his replacement.

As I emptied the contents of my wallet into the shop keepers till (with a light heart – it was a good cause) Oily decided that since June and Sharon were now full time members of our side it was time for them to be properly equipped. So, the whole process began again with the only difference being that this time the recipients of our accumulated wisdom seemed grateful for it. There was some alarm and confusion among the two assistants when Oily reminded Sharon and June that they would need to buy 'protectors' but the embarrassment was overcome and the necessary equipment provided and quickly wrapped.

As we prepared to leave the shop I caught sight of Oily watching the proud young owner of a brand new bat handing over its broken and useless predecessor to one of his companions. The recipient of this largesse seemed delighted. He'd obviously never owned a bat of any sort before and a broken bat was clearly better than no bat at all.

'Would any more of you lads like new bats?' asked Oily, suddenly and unexpectedly.

For a moment there was silence in the shop and then, suddenly, there was chaos and pandemonium as a forest of hands shot skywards and a chorus of tinny voices cried: 'Me!'.

While the two assistants struggled to pull bats off the shelves fast enough for all the budding batsmen Oily slipped out of the shop to cash the cheque he'd received the day before from the Combe Regis captain. By the time he returned, with his pockets full of cash, everyone in the shop was smiling.

* * *

CHAPTER TWELVE

Fresh from our defeat on the beach, and with Wodger's shoes still squelching, we arrived at the North Hawkwater Cricket Club Ground less than half an hour after we had finished an early lunch in a fish and chip cafe on the promenade and with a full hour to spare before our match against the Hawkswater first eleven was due to begin.

Prior to lunch we had watched our beach cricket opponents race back to their waterlogged pitch on the sands. As they ran they waved their brand new bats about them and, armed with so much heavy duty woodwork, made a strangely menacing bunch. We had then returned to the hotel for just long enough to wake up Arthur and to arrange for the hotel staff to move our baggage into such single rooms as had become available. To my delight I discovered that I would be spending my second night at The Royal Grand Atlantic Hotel with at least one partition wall separating my ears from Arthur's snores.

Climbing out of the cars we stretched ourselves in the one small patch of sunshine that was available and looked around.

The North Hawkwater Cricket Club had prepared its ground in a small, oval clearing that was surrounded by a thick boundary of mixed woodland. All around the Ground a mixture of oak, sycamore and beech trees stretched upwards for sixty feet or so. Here and there, through the trees, we caught glimpses of large and impressive looking private houses. To reach the Cricket Club Ground we had had to drive for three quarters of a mile or so along a heavily rutted single track that looked more suitable for tractors than for cars, but the ground's position made the journey well worthwhile. The trees around the clearing isolated us from the world outside and the only sounds we could hear were those of birds singing and squirrels scurrying.

The small pavilion was made entirely of wood and although it was relatively newly built it had been designed according to the traditional Victorian principles. It had a red tiled roof and a raised balcony running along in front of the two dressing rooms and the large centrally situated bar area. A small brass plate attached to the lintel above the front door announced that the pavilion had been built by a Mr. Thomas Winsden.

Our opponents didn't begin to arrive until about a quarter of an hour before the match was scheduled to begin. They were, to say the very least, a mixed bunch. Three arrived in an old, battered Land Rover, one arrived on a bicycle, one arrived in a brand new Rolls Royce and the remainder turned up in the usual mixture of sports and saloon cars. One or two carried large, expensive looking leather sports bags marked with their initials but several had their cricket gear stuffed into plastic carrier bags.

We introduced ourselves to one another, they showed us to our dressing room and we got changed.

When we emerged onto the terrace outside the pavilion to watch Wodger lose the toss we were astonished to see that the ground had become ringed with spectators. Most were sprawled on rugs or simply on the grass but several had brought deck chairs, small tables and picnic hampers.

In our class of cricket we aren't much used to spectators. There are usually half a dozen enthusiasts gathered in front of the pavilion but they are invariably relatives or close friends of the members of the home team. Such support as exists is usually drawn by friendship or loyalty rather than enthusiasm for the game itself or the expected quality of the cricket to be played.

'Spectators!' hissed Norman, whose powers of observation have always been impressive. Nothing much escapes his notice. You cannot ring a small cricket ground with spectators and expect Norman not to notice.

We stood and stared for a few moments at the impressive circle of plaid rugs, pork pies, lemonade bottles, striped canvas deck chairs and the other inevitable impedimenta associated with cricket watching. There was even a small contingent of first aid experts sitting next to the tent they'd pitched to the left of the pavilion.

For a moment or two none of us spoke but I could tell that the others felt as uncomfortable as I did in the face of this massed expression of interest. Somehow spectators make a match seem more serious and more important than it is. Without any spectators you can miss a catch, bowl a wide or step on your wicket without any real sense of embarrassment. Other cricketers will usually ignore such trivial errors. After a moment or two everyone will have forgotten. Another over will start, another batsman will take strike and the game will go on. Unpleasant memories can be erased or pleasantly distorted. Without spectators there to remind you of the truth (and to remind you that by their very presence the truth cannot be suppressed) it is possible to disguise or rearrange the past so that it becomes more acceptable.

Without spectators it is possible to make your batting errors a consequence of misfortune rather than any lack of skill or application. The ball hit a stone on the wicket. The run out was someone else's fault. The wind blew the bails off. The bowler came out of the trees. The sightscreen was in the wrong place. The umpire was short sighted, long sighted or ignorant of the new LBW law. The catch was taken off your elbow. The ball bounced off the wicket keeper's pads. These excuses are as commonplace as they are numerous. They are a normally accepted part of the game; as necessary and as inevitable as the tales the fisherman tells of the one that got away. So vital are these simple reorganisations of history that everyone else in the team will help you convince yourself that your imagination is more accurate than the truth.

Spectators destroy all this. Spectators are a living and constant reminder of incompetence and frailty.

It's all right for professionals to have to put up with spectators. They are paid to feel incompetent and frail. But however honoured and flattered we may be by their presence we club cricketers do not really like spectators. They make us too vulnerable to shame and expose us to the embarrassment that is too often associated with the truth.

And the first aid tent didn't help either.

Cricket is not usually a particularly dangerous game. But nothing is guaranteed to remind players of the hazards more effectively than the presence of a St John's Ambulance representative or a Red Cross worker.

Drive at seventy miles an hour down the motorway and you will feel secure and safe from harm until you see an accident – or even an ambulance. The sight of all that mangled metal and blood, or the vision of an ambulance hurrying someone in pain to hospital, is an instant reminder of just how fragile the human body is.

Similarly, the sight to a first aid tent is an effective reminder of bruises, fractures and bloody noses.

A friend of mine who had been in London for a gloomy meeting with a solicitor (he was arranging his own bankruptcy) once popped into Lords to try and soak up some of the atmosphere and cheer himself up. But he claims that it was the most miserable and frightening experience of his life. He says that the few hours he spent at Lords frightened him more than the visit to the solicitors.

Although it was a sunny, warm and pleasant day he says that they didn't actually play any cricket. He says the umpires kept coming out, studying the grass very carefully and then going back into the pavilion again.

He says they must have gone out onto the field at least half a dozen times to have a look around and wave to the spectators. He says he wondered at the time if they were just waiting to see if enough spectators came to make it worth while playing. In the end he says that a man in a light raincoat told him that they were trying to decide whether the grass was too wet or too dry, too short or too long. He says that the man told him that they have to look after the grass at Lords to make sure that it's always kept in good condition.

My friend says that in the end all the excitement of wondering whether or not there was going to be any cricket seemed to have got to one of the spectators for the loudspeaker announcer suddenly interrupted the silence to ask Dr Roberts to go to the first aid post. My friend says that he was impressed to hear that they had a doctor on call at a cricket match and that for a few minutes he felt strangely reassured. He says that he walked round the ground in a very carefree state of mind, knowing that Dr Roberts would be there to look after him should he fall ill.

The good feeling didn't last long, however, for a few minutes later the loudspeaker announcer again broke the silence with another request. This time he simply asked for a doctor – any doctor – to go to the first aid post.

It was, says my friend, a trifle disappointing to know that Dr Roberts wasn't on the ground but he consoled himself with the thought that Dr Roberts' patients were probably being well looked after somewhere else in London. Anyway, he says, it was nice to know that the ground announcer had confidence that there would be a doctor of some kind among the spectators. He says he wasn't quite as confident as he had been when he thought that Dr Roberts was around because he had got to trust Dr Roberts but that he still felt quite happy about things. He says it was like being in hospital as a visitor, knowing that if you fell over or got hit by a porter with a runaway trolley there would be expert help available immediately. After a moment or two he says he even began to feel pleased that Dr Roberts hadn't bothered to turn up since it was clear that there wouldn't really be any need for him. He says he had a vision of a dozen eminent specialists scrambing towards the first aid post to offer their expert advice and support.

Sadly, that sense of comfort didn't last very long because about five minutes later there was a third appeal. This time the announcer sounded a little more worried. He asked for a nurse to go to the first aid post just as soon as possible. My friend says that he found this chilling. He says he suddenly became very worried and couldn't help wondering what was happening at the first aid post and why there wasn't a doctor around. He claims he went quite cold with fear and stopped eating the pasty he had bought himself in case he choked on it. He says he's never felt quite so ill or so frightened in his life.

When, a few more minutes later, the announcer came back on to beg anyone with any first aid experience to go directly to the first aid post my friend had had enough. He put down his pasty and walked slowly and carefully out of the ground. He says he had never been so relieved to leave anywhere in his life and that it was only when he got outside that he began to breathe properly again. According to him being at Lords that day was like being sentenced to a slow, lingering and painful death and he still says that he wouldn't have stayed in there a moment longer even if they'd started playing cricket.

*　　*　　*

CHAPTER THIRTEEN

We began to see why the spectators had turned up when Wodger lost the toss and we found ourselves asked to bat first.

The man who opened the bowling for the home side was about a foot taller than anyone else on the field. He had huge black, bushy eyebrows and a large, straggly black moustache that covered his mouth entirely. He was built rather like a small apartment building and when he began his first, long, determined run up to the wicket I was sure I could feel the ground underneath me shaking even though he was sixty to seventy yards away from us at the time. The top of his head was almost entirely bald but he had a fringe of thick black hair at the back of his head which waved and danced in the breeze as he ran in to deliver his first ball.

'Is he fast?' Brian asked the nearest spectator, a plump, middle aged woman who was managing to butter endless slices of bread without taking her eyes off the cricket.

'You'll see!' said the woman without moving her eyes or breaking her buttering stroke.

At this point I should perhaps mention that no one in our side ever wears a helmet.

There are two reasons for this.

First, in our class of cricket we don't usually come up against bowlers who are menacing enough to make helmets essential.

And second, we can't afford them.

Oily did buy a helmet when they first became popular but I think he felt bad about being the only member of the side to wear one. He offered to lend it to the rest of us but Oily's head is so large that for most of us it was like trying to bat while wearing a coal bucket. On the single occasion when I tried to bat in it I found that unless I kept my head tilted backwards all the time I couldn't see anything at all. Eventually, partly through a wish to help maintain the team spirit but mainly through a sense of embarrassment, Oily abandoned his helmet.

The sound of a cricket ball hitting a skull always makes me cringe.

On this occasion I didn't see the ball at all. One moment Wodger was standing, gently tapping his bat in his crease. The next moment he was lying flat on his back and a fielder was running in from fine leg to catch the ball. The wicket keeper and umpire later insisted that the ball had merely caught Wodger's head a glancing blow before flying off down the leg side but the sound we heard suggested a more definitive impact.

Cricket injuries fall into two distinct categories. On the one hand there are the injuries which produce laughter rather than sympathy. Into this category I would put anything which involves an umpire's ankle or a batsman's groin. On the other hand there are the injuries which produce a feeling of nausea deep in the stomach of anyone who is watching at the time. There is no doubt that Wodger's injury fell into the second category.

Alarmed by the sound we had heard when the ball hit Wodger's head Oily and I both ran onto the pitch to join the huddle of players and umpires which had quickly gathered around our stricken captain. There was blood everywhere.

'How is he?' I asked no one in particular and immediately felt foolish. What a stupid question. Why do we ask these things?

'He's been hit on the head,' said one of the umpires, equally usefully.

Oily and I knelt down beside Wodger's head. The wicket keeper and another fielder had already moved Wodger onto his side so that he didn't swallow his tongue. The blood had already spread onto his shirt, trousers, pads and bat. Several fielders were also spattered with blood, as were the stumps. The wicket keeper, who seemed to be in charge, had folded a linen handkerchief into a small pad and was using it to help stop the bleeding. He kept his thumb pressed on the pad as he turned towards us. He was about to speak when Wodger, who looked whiter than I ever imagined any human being could be without dying, suddenly groaned and tried to lift an arm up to his head.

'He'll be OK,' said the wicket keeper. 'But we'd better get him to the hospital for an X ray.'

As though to justify the wicket keeper's prognosis Wodger groaned again and opened his eyes. He blinked for a moment or two, looked up at Oily and I and tried to smile.

'Lost sight of it in the trees,' he said apologetically.

The two first aiders, who had by now joined us all, bent down and lifted Wodger onto the stretcher which they'd brought with them. One of them took a bandage out of the satchel which was slung around his neck and used it to hold the wicket keeper's padded handkerchief firmly pressed against Wodger's scalp.

'I'll be all right in a couple of minutes,' insisted Wodger, waving an arm around and nearly falling off the stretcher. He opened his eyes again and blinked once more. 'I think the ball must have kicked on a spike mark,' he said. 'It reared up a bit.'

'They're taking you to hospital for a precautionary X ray,' I told him. It was a phrase I'd heard before and even though I'd said it I found it strangely reassuring. I hoped Wodger was equally calmed and comforted by it. 'I'll come with you.'

Wodger tried to smile again, closed his eyes and folded his arms across his stomach. Someone handed me his bat to carry.

The first aiders moved towards their tent with commendable speed and efficiency and once there carefully lifted Wodger into the back of a capacious Ford van which was parked nearby.

*   *   *

The doctors at the local hospital were very good. They X-rayed Wodger, dressed his wound and took him along to the ward where they insisted he would have to stay for 24 hours observation.

'You get back to the match!' Wodger told me. 'But watch out for the uneven bounce – that's what caught me out.'

I promised that I would, told him we'd be back to see him that evening and found a taxi outside the hospital to take me back to the North Hawkwater Cricket Club Ground. The two first aiders had hurried back to the ground the moment they'd deposited their patient in the casualty department. They said they didn't like to be away for too long in case they were needed.

'He's a bit shaken and the doctors say he'll have a headache for a day or two but he'll be OK,' I told the others when I got back. 'I said we'd call in and see him after the match.'

'You're just in time,' said Jerry, who had his left arm wrapped in a makeshift sling. 'We moved you right down the batting order but you're in next.'

'What's the score?' I asked.

'We're 62 for 8,' said Oily who was sitting on the pavilion steps with one foot resting in a bowl of water.

'It's the dentist who's doing all the damage,' said Norman. 'He's a bit out of our league.'

Norman had a large swelling just under his left eye and some dried blood on his upper lip which suggested that he'd suffered a nose bleed.

'Which dentist?'

'The fast bowler with the moustache and the eyebrows,' said the vicar. I looked at him carefully but could see no sign of injury.

'You seem to be OK,' I said. 'Congratulations!'

Ruefully the vicar held up his left hand and showed me the massive bruise developing around his left wrist.

'It's been like a battlefield out there,' said June, showing me a huge bruise developing on the inside of her right thigh.

'Apparently we're doing quite well,' said Brian, who opened his mouth to show me his broken tooth. 'The last team who played here had four of its top six batsmen out of action within the first half an hour.'

'It reminds me of a match I once played in Yorkshire,' said Oily, lifting his foot out of the bowl and inspecting it for a moment before plunging it back into the water again. 'The home side had an opening bowler who'd just heard that

99

he'd been turned down for the county side. He was furious and determined to take it out on someone.'

'I heard someone say that the dentist had been offered a county trial but had said 'no',' said the vicar, rubbing his wrist carefully. 'Apparently he said he didn't want to take the game too seriously.'

'Sharon's just got a nice two,' said June, nodding towards the wicket. We watched as Sharon and Arthur ran another surprisingly quick two runs.

'One of our opening batsmen got hit on the side of the head by a rising ball that just clipped the shoulder of his bat,' continued Oily. 'It hit him just above the eye and second slip leapt and took a good catch a yard and a half to his right.'

'That's 64 for 8,' said Norman. 'Sharon's our top scorer now – apart from extras – she's just got into double figures.'

'She's very good, isn't she?' said the vicar.

'Terrific!' said Simon. It was so unusual to hear his voice that we all turned and looked at him. He blushed bright red. He was, I noticed, carefully massaging his right thumb which looked swollen and sore. 'Great!' He said. He looked around and went even redder. 'At cricket, I mean,' he finished lamely.

'By the time the chap had caught it our batsman was lying flat on his back on the ground,' continued Oily, refusing to abandon his anecdote.

'I think Simon's getting a bit fond of young Sharon,' grinned Brian. He looked across at Oily. 'You'll have to watch out!' he said, with a wink. His broken tooth gave him a slightly piratical look.

'The thing was,' said Oily, ignoring the interruption, 'the thing was that our chap was stone dead.' He looked around to make sure that we'd heard him. We all made suitably sympathetic noises for the batsmen we'd never known.

'So there was a terrible fuss,' Oily went on. 'The bowler reckoned that since the catch was a clean one the batsman was out but the umpire reckoned that you can't give out a batsman who's already dead. He said that as far as he was concerned the batsman had retired hurt the moment he'd died and since he'd died instantaneously he'd retired before he'd been caught.' Oily shook his head at the memory of it all.

'Terrible fuss there was. It lasted for ages.'

'I think the bowler probably had a point,' said the vicar after a moment or two's silent thought. 'I wouldn't have thought ...'

'Arthur's out!' said Jerry suddenly. We all watched as Arthur began the long, slow trudge back to the pavilion.

'What happened?' asked Norman.

'Caught at mid-on trying his usual,' replied Jerry, referring to the fact that Arthur's favourite (and some say only) shot is a rural hoik that lacks grace but has scored him a considerable number of runs over the years.

'You're in!' Oily reminded me.

'And the dentist's coming back on,' said June. 'So watch out!'

With my heart fluttering rather faster than usual I hurriedly fastened my pads, picked up my bat and gloves and began the long walk out to the middle.

As I dragged my bat behind me I looked up at the sky, hoping that there might be a few rain clouds overhead. Why, I wondered, does rain never come when you want it?

And why, I wondered, are dentists always so frightening?

I once knew a dentist socially. I met him at dinner parties a couple of times and got to know him quite well. He told me that apart from looking after his normal patients he also had the job of caring for the inmates of a large local prison.

Most of the prisoners had apparently had their teeth removed informally in public houses, quiet moonlit car parks and confidential corners of prison exercise yards but there were, he said, one or two prisoners who needed to have teeth removed in a more organised manner.

According to my acquaintance, criminals as a group tend to practise poor dental hygiene. He said he thought it was probably understandable. 'If you're rushing around with a stocking over your face and a sawn off shotgun in your hands,' he said, 'you probably don't get much chance to sit around in dentists' waiting rooms. Besides, when you're face is covered up with a stocking you probably don't worry too much about your appearance.'

On one particular occasion my dental acquaintance found himself removing half a dozen blackened and decaying stumps from the well photographed jaws of a convicted bank robber who had, just a few months before, been pictured on notice-boards outside police stations as far apart as Aberdeen and Weymouth.

'Despite my skill,' said my dental acquaintance modestly, 'the sockets from which I'd removed his rotten teeth wouldn't stop bleeding. After trying to stop the flow of blood for half and hour or so I decided I'd have to take him to the prison hospital for more sophisticated treatment.'

To get to the prison hospital the small party, consisting of the dentist, the inevitable pretty assistant, the prisoner and two large prison officers, had to go along a corridor which just happened that day to be filled with a group of visiting social workers and student probation officers.

Never one to miss a chance to display his dark sense of humour my dental acquaintance grabbed the bank robber by the arm as they walked along the corridor and said, in a loud stage whisper: 'Now, will you tell us where the damned money is hidden?'

The prisoner, with blood dribbling down his chin and his mouth numb with anaesthetic, was quite unable to reply to this unexpected query.

According to my acquaintance the social workers and student probation officers rose to this bait as speedily as a hungry trout will rise to an illicit worm on a pleasant summer evening. The Governor of the prison had to organise a full inquiry and my dentist friend eventually found himself relieved of his onerous responsibilities at the prison.

'How's Wodger?' asked Sharon, as I strode towards the wicket. I was doing my best to disguise my nervousness but I suspect I may not have been too successful.

'Wodger?' I heard myself saying. 'Wodger who?'

'Wodger,' said Sharon. 'The captain ... I thought you went to the hospital with him ...'

'Oh, *that* Wodger!' I said. 'He'll be OK. He's staying the night.'

Sharon was at the striker's end when the dentist began his new over. He clearly intended it to be his last over and did not seem disposed to bowl slowly to Sharon, as I'd rather hoped he would. With some reluctance but little choice I agreed to take a bye off the first ball. It was the only option for anyone with any hope of maintaining any shred of a reputation as a gentleman.

I had watched the dentist's delivery as carefully as I could, hoping that I might learn something from my observation.

Unfortunately, I had learnt nothing; largely because I did not even see the ball.

Even before he had begun his run up for the second delivery of the over I had decided that I had little alternative but to hit out and hope for the best. With any luck I would be bowled first ball.

I don't know which one of us was most surprised – the dentist or myself – when my full blooded drive connected full blade with the ball and sent it firing straight back down the wicket.

The crack the ball made as it hit the dentist's ankle must have been heard by every spectator on the ground. It sounded like a rifle shot. And the dentist fell to the ground as quickly as if he'd been hit by a rifle shot.

After that our innings was an anti-climax. The bowler who finished the dentist's over bowled two long hops which I was lucky enough to dispatch to the boundary and then yorked me with a slower ball.

We were 73 all out.

When, after the tea interval, it was our turn to take the field we suddenly realised that we had a problem: we had no captain.

Our normal vice captain, Sergeant Tate, had still not re-appeared (which was just as well since his wife and the vicar had now developed a firmly established relationship) and so when we wandered onto the field we did so with no leader.

Eventually, we decided that Norman should take on the job. I can't imagine why we chose Norman since we all knew that he is constitutionally incapable of making a decision but it probably seemed a good idea at the time. And as things turned out it didn't make much difference anyway. Exactly an hour after the North Hawkwater eleven started their innings the heavens opened, the pitch flooded, the spectators dispersed into the trees and we abandoned the match as a draw.

We were, I suspect, lucky to get away with a draw. They had scored 70 without loss at the time and would probably claim that they were destined for victory.

*   *   *

CHAPTER FOURTEEN

I'd never seen rain like it before. One moment the sky was blue and the air warmed by summer sunshine. The next moment huge puddles were spreading across the wicket and turning the outfield into a small boating lake. One moment the spectators around the boundary's edge were lying back enjoying the sunshine, the next moment they were scurrying for shelter under the trees.

We'd changed and packed our gear and were staring out at our cars from the safety of the pavilion when the North Hawkwater captain came in to congratulate us, to ask us to pass on his best wishes to Wodger and to tell us that he hoped we'd come back another year. He had to shout to make himself heard above the sound of the rain crashing down onto the pavilion roof.

We all shook his hand, congratulated him and promised to take his good wishes to Wodger. Then we shook hands with the dentist and the rest of the home side and finally we squeezed out onto the tiny balcony. The rain was, if anything, getting worse.

Our cars were parked only a few yards away but by the time we reached them we were all soaked to the skin.

We nearly didn't get away from the ground that evening. I suspect that if we'd left it any longer we'd have been stuck there for the night. The rain had turned the rutted track that led back through the woods towards the main road into a quagmire. But eventually we made it. And from North Hawkwater we set off for the local hospital to see how Wodger was getting on.

By the time we found the hospital the rain had stopped almost as suddenly as it had started. There were large puddles everywhere but the sky was bright. A huge, double-ended rainbow arched over the horizon like a multi-coloured bridge.

Wodger was sitting up in bed explaining to two nurses how he'd been temporarily blinded by a flash of sunlight on a camera lens and had mistimed a hook shot. He blushed when he saw us approaching but we weren't about to spoil his fun.

'How are you captain?' asked Oily. 'You looked set for a big innings before the accident.'

Wodger blushed a deeper red and the two nurses blew him kisses as they crept away.

'I'll be out in the morning,' Wodger assured us. 'They're only keeping me in for observation.'

'You have to be careful with head injuries,' warned Norman. 'They can be very nasty.'

'I had an uncle . . .' began Norman.

And we were off.

Why is it, I wonder, that everyone is an authority on medical matters?

If a fellow in a pub mentions the bankruptcy laws or the significance of black holes or the role of genetic engineering in modern society there will be yawns all round and someone will call for another round.

But if anyone mentions illness or disease everyone present will have something to say on the matter. There will be long winded anecdotes, diagnostic tips, details of suitable drugs, alternative remedies and heaven knows what else. Everyone is an expert on medicine and I never fail to be surprised at the number of people who, without any formal medical training, are able to solve problems that have defied the attention of thousands of highly skilled scientists.

How many people do you know who can keep quiet when the subject of the common cold crops up? How many people do you know who can resist the temptation to offer their own pet theories and to bore sufferers with their advice?

When Norman finally concluded his anecdote (which as far as I could tell concerned an uncle of his who was hit on the head by a cricket ball when he was seven and died 84 years later as a direct result of the injury) Jerry told us about his grandmother who once went into hospital to have an ingrowing toe nail seen to and narrowly escaped having her right leg amputated.

Brian then told us the story of his mum. He always tells this story whenever the conversation turns to anything medical. I've heard the story at least a dozen times now and I can join in with the chorus where necessary but since you probably haven't heard it its probably worth relating.

Brian's mum had been 'under the doctor' as she puts it for twenty years and officially she was a patient of one of our most eminent local senior consultants. She never saw him, however, since he was always far too busy sitting on committees and looking after his private patients. Instead, Brian's mum was looked after by an apparently endless series of young trainee doctors. She'd visited the hospital twice a year for twenty years and had probably been seen by forty different doctors.

For nearly all of that time Brian's mum was quite a problem patient. She suffered from two separate disorders – diabetes and high blood pressure – and her hospital medical records showed that when one disease was under control the other would almost always be out of control. It seemed that the doctors just couldn't control both of her problems at once. Her other major problem was her weight which, according to the hospital scales, went up and down quite inexplicably.

Faced with what they regarded as an insoluble clinical problem the young doctors who looked after Brian's mum had, over the years, tried just about every possible combination of treatments.

They had put her on reducing diets, they had given her slimming pills, they had given her calorie lists and they had recommended exercises. In an attempt to control her diabetes they had prescribed insulin, special tablets and sugar free diets. To deal with her blood pressure problem they had tried relaxation classes, diuretics and all sorts of expensive and wonderful therapeutic solutions.

None of it worked. Sometimes they told her that her blood

pressure was lower than before. But then, the next time, they'd tell her that it had gone up. Sometimes, her diabetes seemed to be very well controlled. And then, within months, it would be out of control again.

Brian's mum was never seriously ill but she was never seriously well either. She was never ill enough to be admitted to the hospital for treatment but she was never well enough to be discharged from the clinic. She looked like being a patient for life.

In the end it was the thickness of Brian's mum's medical records folder which eventually led to a solution.

The number of notes that had been written about her grew to such extraordinary proportions that a junior clerk in the medical records department was given the task of tidying them up.

Fortunately for Brian's mum and several future generations of young doctors the young clerk who was chosen to tidy up the notes was sharp enough to notice that Brian's mum seemed to have two quite different addresses. When she came and was overweight and rather severely diabetic she lived in a small council flat on the North side of the town. But when she was slender and had blood pressure trouble she lived in a rather large house in the East.

It turned out that for twenty years Brian's mum had shared a set of medical records with another patient with a similar name. Although they were quite definitely two they were treated as one. The lack of medical continuity meant that no one noticed anything wrong.

Between them Brian's mum and her unofficial twin illustrate vividly the astonishing ability of the human body to put up with the unnecessary drugs, unwanted treatments, pointless diets and needless advice offered by a bottomless hamper of enthusiastic young medical assistants.

There was suddenly a loud thud as the patient next to Wodger fell out of his bed and crashed to the floor.

The noise he made attracted the ward sister who was alarmed and appalled to see so many of us gathered around one bed. She threw us out.

After promising to return the following morning to pick Wodger up we made our way back to the hotel where we spent an uneventful evening playing poor snooker and drinking our way through the barman's speciality list of rare and exotic cocktails.

* * *

CHAPTER FIFTEEN

We'd been told that we could pick up Wodger at eleven the following morning (after the consultant in charge had seen him) and so after breakfast we had an hour or two with nothing much to do.

Norman decided to get a hair cut and Oily and I offered to go with him to hunt for a hairdressers. To be honest we both thought that a little fresh air would do us good. The cocktails we'd drunk the night before might have been well mixed but they didn't mix well.

Personally, I've always felt that there are two sorts of people in the world and that it is possible to tell which category someone is in by his response when you've got a hangover.

On the one hand there are the folk who sniff in a very superior way and make it pretty clear that you're not to expect any sympathy at all from them because you have got exactly what you deserve if you will go out drinking, debauching and generally having a good time. These are, I suspect, the same cheerful, self righteous citizens who always look smug and self satisfied when anyone confesses to some minor problem. Tell them that you're broke and they let you know straight away that anyone who doesn't take care of his money is a wastrel and a scoundrel. Get a girl into trouble or catch a nasty and unfortunate social disease and you can see them positively glowing with self appointed superiority and full of that very special type of satisfaction enjoyed by people who like saying 'I told you so'.

People in this category enjoy other people's misery. The greater the agony and the deeper the misery the better they feel. They're complacent, cautious and boring. They buy their

Christmas cards in the January sales and they always carry those little sewing kits in their briefcases in case a button comes loose. They go through life as though they have rented their bodies and have to get them back in tip top condition. They never, ever get hangovers.

I've always been warmed by the conviction that people in this category suffer a lot with their nerves and get a lot of indigestion and wind.

There was a time, I have to confess, when I would have put Norman into this category of individual. But I'm pleased to say that in the last year or two he has become a decent enough fellow – particularly for an accountant. He always manages to look innocent and rather surprised when he finds himself vomiting in the street but he does it often enough to know how far to bend over so that he'll keep his shoes clean.

In the second category I would put those gentle and sympathetic souls who always greet news of misfortune with sympathy, compassion, understanding and a feeling of 'there but for the Grace of God go I'.

People in this category always lower their voices when they know you've got a hangover. And they can nearly always give you details of their own very special hangover remedy.

The chap who looks after my teeth is a great hair of the dog man. He claims that scientists have shown that hangovers are only produced when blood alcohol levels fall below a certain point. His favourite remedy is to take the juice out of half a bottle of scotch, add a tablespoonful of honey and a handful of crushed ice and then sip the resulting mixture through a straw. He insists that the ice has to be crushed because crushed ice is the only sort that doesn't make a clinking noise when it hits the side of the glass.

My cousin, on the other hand, is an exercise advocate. He says that the best way to get rid of a hangover is to sweat it out and to achieve this end he does some pretty extraordinary things. I once found him outside in the garden trying to do 100 press ups with an old car battery balanced on his backside. Once, when it had been snowing, he went outside in his swimming trunks and rolled over and over until he went quite blue with cold. He insisted that they do it all the

111

time in Sweden. All I can say is that the police in Sweden must be a lot more tolerant than they are here for he got fined £35 and given a conditional discharge for causing a breach of the peace.

Jerry always swears by some funny little pills he buys from a small shop in Bristol. I don't think that even he knows precisely what they contain but, according to the label, they include more ingredients than the average Christmas cake.

The ingredients are all mixed up together and then packaged in capsules that look like horse pills. Jerry always carries two of his pills with him in a small metal box. The pills are so large that two is all the box will contain.

Jerry once gave me one to try when we'd been up in Yorkshire for a charity cricket match and I don't think I've ever felt so ill as I did afterwards. On balance I think I'd prefer a hangover to one of Jerry's pills.

So, the three of us tiptoed out of the hotel and strolled gently along the promenade looking for a hairdressers.

Norman hasn't got all that much hair and what there is tends to be concentrated at the back of his head but he gets a little edgy if it isn't trimmed regularly. He is a great believer in habits and reckons they are the framework upon which any life is built. Take away a man's habits, I've heard him say, and you take away the man. He can, he claims, tell everything he needs to know about a man by learning about his habits. He says, for example, that he would never trust a man who adjusts his trousers before crossing his legs. He insists that if you go into the waiting room outside any bankruptcy court you will see row upon row of men all carefully adjusting their creases before crossing their legs.

At home Norman always goes to the barbers that he's patronised since he was a boy but in Newquay we found that local alternatives were rather sparse. After searching through the usual vast array of building society offices and shoe shops we eventually stopped and asked a traffic warden if she knew where we could find a barber. To our relief and Norman's delight she told us that there was one just round the corner from where we were standing.

Maybe I'm old fashioned but in my heart I know what I expect when I look for a barbers. I want the floor to be covered with cracked, brown linoleum and I want it to be covered with a thick matting of cut hair. I want chairs covered in red plastic and I want semi clad models staring down from out of date calendars pinned to walls which have the paint peeling from them. I want bottles of brilliantine and toothpaste sharing shelves with rows of 'anything else for the weekend, sir?' and I want a collection of tabloid newspapers scattered over the chairs for customers who are waiting.

Standing in the middle of this comforting and comfortable landscape there will be three or four middle aged men in white coats. Each man will be equipped with a comb, a hair brush with a well worn wooden handle, a wooden framed mirror with a long, rounded, wooden handle, a pair of scissors which seem inseparable from his fingers and a pair of electrically powered black clippers with which to attack the small hairs at the back of the customer's neck.

The customer (and he is quite definitely a customer and not a patron or a client) sits in one of the large, red plastic covered chairs and watches the whole operation in a large, rather mottled mirror which carries several stick on advertisements for the products which adorn the shelves of the accompanying cupboards. A jar of long spills will stand in front of the mirror so that the barber can give his more mature clients a singe.

In this haven of peace the customer waits for somewhere between fifteen and twenty minutes to take his turn in the chair. There is no appointment system. Before the barber starts work the customer spends about thirty seconds saying something like 'the usual' or 'a little off the top and sides, please'. While this conversation is going on the barber will be tying a large white sheet around the customer's neck. If the barber and the customer know one another well then this part of the conversation may be omitted.

During the cutting of the hair, which takes no less than ten and no more than fifteen minutes, the barber is authorised to make three attempts in initiate a conversation. He will mention the weather, make a vague comment about the local football team and ask the customer whether or not he is busy for the time of the year.

The customer thus has three chances to decide whether or

113

not he wants to be entertained while his hair is cut. If he wants to sit quietly for the duration of the hair cut he has only to reply in crisp, short sentences to these questions. The barber will understand and shut up. If the customer wants to chat then he can easily do so by making some reciprocal comments about the weather, the local football team or business for the time of the year. The conversation, once initiated, can follow any direction selected by the customer.

When the hair cutting ritual is over the barber will hold up his mirror behind the customer's head so that the back view can be examined. The customer must then nod his approval, whatever he feels about the success or otherwise of the enterprise. The barber then sprays a weak but potent cologne over the customer's head, removes the white sheet and offers the customer a small paper towel so that he can wipe away the small hairs that have managed to get down the back of his neck. While the customer is doing this the barber will, with the aid of a raised eyebrow, ask the customer if he wants 'anything else for the weekend'. The barber will then walk across to the till and wait for the customer to dig out the requisite amount of change.

Men have always had their hair cut this way. I firmly believe that even back in the middle ages, when barbers doubled as surgeons and would trim off a gangrenous leg as readily as they would trim an errant curl, they must have had red plastic chairs, brown, cracked linoleum and packets of 'anything else for the weekend, sir?' stacked in glass fronted cupboards.

In Newquay, however, we found ourselves in something calling itself a Unisex Hairdressers.

It was an experience we all found unnerving.

The floor was thickly carpeted in something soft and pale green, the walls were decorated with Japanese prints while potted palms and hanging vines served to give the place an uncomfortably horticultural look. Hidden loudspeakers filled the whole place with an uninspired and uninspiring sound and a small army of unisex hairdressers wandered about dressed in jeans and sweatshirts.

'Does unisex refer to the customers or the staff?' asked Oily in a stage whisper.

'Ssshhh!' said Norman, embarrassed.

114

'Konielpyew?'

We heard it but didn't understand it. Nor did we know where it had come from.

The sound was repeated and we slowly realised that it was coming from a blonde girl wearing a light green smock who was sitting behind a huge desk and almost entirely hidden behind a wall of potted plants.

'Konielpyew?' repeated the girl.

'I'd like a hair cut,' said Norman.

'Evyewgotanapphointmunt?'

We looked at one another in despair.

She repeated what was clearly a question.

'Oh!' said Oily, suddenly understanding. 'An appointment?'

'An appointment?' said Norman, puzzled.

I shared his distress. To find a barber demanding that the customers make appointments is rather like finding a petrol station that won't sell petrol to motorists who haven't booked a space at the pumps or finding a landlord who isn't prepared to serve beer to customers who haven't booked a bar stool.

Norman explained that he only wanted a hair cut.

The girl looked unhappy, sniffed and studied her diary carefully. 'Yewerlucky,' she said. 'Thursacancullashun.'

'You're from Walsall, aren't you?' said Oily.

The girl looked startled. 'Owjuno?' she demanded.

Oily smiled and shrugged. The girl glowered at him.

'Yewllavtewaitoutside,' she announced firmly, looking at Oily and myself.

And so while Norman stayed behind to get his hair cut Oily and I wandered back outside onto the streets to see what joys Newquay had to offer us.

*   *   *

The first thing we saw when we came out of the hairdressing salon was one of those crazy golf courses which are such a feature of seaside resorts these days. Neither Oily nor I could resist it.

We are such keen golf enthusiasts that we once took a few days off work to go and watch a professional golf tournament in Scotland.

When we set off we'd thought we would be able to find

a pleasant little hotel with its own trout stream where we could start each day with a huge breakfast of bacon, sausage, kidneys and scrambled eggs; all served by buxom, good looking country girls dressed in pink gingham and all wide eyed, giggly and innocent.

Oily described the hotel first of all as we were driving up the motorway. He was confident that we wouldn't have any difficulty in finding it. He assured me that in view of the breakfasts we would be eating we would have to cut down on luncheons and dinner but he said it would be well worthwhile.

We got our first indication that things might not go quite as smoothly as we had expected when, about twenty miles south of the course, we found ourselves stuck in an enormous traffic jam. That didn't worry us too much at first because we felt that a few hours in a traffic jam was a small price to pay for the joy of staying in a small and comfortable Scottish country hotel. We were full of good spirits and after about forty minutes we got quite friendly with the foursome in the car in front who were also heading north to watch the golf.

We told the foursome about the hotel we were going to stay at because they seemed quite decent blokes and we thought they might like to join us. To our amazement we discovered that all four of them had already decided that they would stop at exactly the same place and that they would have their massive country breakfasts served by the same fresh faced country girls in a dining room that had pink gingham curtains and a view of the twelfth green.

There was some slight disagreement over this last point because Oily and I were convinced that our hotel would have a trout stream outside the dining room window. Eventually, we settled our differences by agreeing that our hotel would have a trout stream and theirs a view of the twelfth green.

After we'd been sitting in the traffic jam for an hour and a half we got quite friendly with the couple in the car behind and found that they were too were looking forward to spending a few days in a similar hotel. They said that they were particularly looking forward to it because they suspected that the bar would be exceptionally well stocked with a good variety of malt whiskies. They said that from their bedrooms they would be able to see the outline of a distillery. They agreed that there would be sausages, bacon, kidneys and eggs for breakfast but said that they probably wouldn't be able to do the food justice because they would be eating too much freshly caught trout.

Oily and I got to the village where the tournament was due to be held at about ten that evening and we drove round and round for another two hours looking for the hotel we'd set our hearts on. Our first major disappointment was finding that there was no such hotel in the neighbourhood. Our second major disappointment was discovering that the hotels that did exist were all fully booked. We spent the night in the car and for breakfast shared a bottle of milk which we bought from a passing farmer and a packet of mints which Oily found in the glove compartment of the car.

The one big advantage we did have was that we didn't have far to travel to get to the course the following morning. We'd managed to park in a lay-by near to the course entrance and consequently we didn't have much driving to do to get to the tournament.

Both Oily and I were pretty excited about it all. We couldn't decide whether to go round the course with one of the big name international stars or simply to stay at one of the greens and watch all the action there. We thought we'd try a bit of both.

Unfortunately, that turned out to be something of a mistake because every time we went to try and watch something we found ourselves at the back of a huge crowd. We bought cardboard periscopes which worked all right for a while but a short, sharp shower made the cardboard soggy and meant that eventually we ended up getting a very good view of our own feet.

Eventually, towards mid-day we wandered back to the tented village that surrounded the club house and managed to bribe an official to let us go round to the back of the press tent. There we found a small gap in the canvas and took it in turns to look through and watch the play on a television screen. Between us we managed to watch most of the good matches and we got a far better view than if we'd struggled round the course.

That evening we tried to find ourselves a hotel again but

failed and at ten o'clock decided that enough was enough so we'd head for home. In the queue away from the area we found ourselves next to the foursome we'd met on our way up to the match. We didn't like to admit that things hadn't gone quite as planned so we told them that we'd decided to leave early because the hotel food was so rich that we feared for our lives. We said that the breakfasts there were so vast that we simply wouldn't have been able to eat two in the same week.

The foursome said they'd had much the same problem at their hotel and that the view of the twelfth green had been so idyllic that they hadn't wanted to stay too long for fear that they would eventually spoil themselves for all other views.

That was our only experience of a professional golf tournament. It was, we both decided ten minutes later, more fun than playing round the crazy golf course.

Once we'd abandoned the golf course we decided we'd find ourselves a quiet little cafe, drink some tea and munch some buttered toast until it was time to collect Norman and head back for the hotel.

*　　*　　*

Fifteen minutes later, as I greedily thrust the last corner of buttered toast into my mouth I noticed that Oily seemed to be fascinated by something that was happening across the street from the Olde Devon Cafe. His fingers were poised mere inches from his mouth but a knob of butter was sliding inexorably towards the edge of his slice of toast. Without losing my masticatory stride I watched the butter drop slowly onto his shirt front and then followed his gaze across the street.

I don't know what the building was. It could have been a library, a health centre or a collection of council offices. It had that grey, dull, concrete look of an *official* building. Whatever its function the architect had clearly been influenced by the needs of the infirm and the disabled for he had arranged for a ramp to be built between the pavement and the front door so that people in wheel chairs could gain access to the building.

Unfortunately, the architect's good intentions had not been

matched by his intelligence for the door at the top of the ramp opened outwards. The result of this simple but vital error was that the crippled visitor who had captured Oily's attention was now stuck half way up the ramp with his hand on the door handle and no way to move any further up the ramp. If he tried to pull the door open he would have to roll back down the ramp to the pavement. But without moving his wheelchair he couldn't open the door. It was a cruel impasse.

While we both watched the man in the wheelchair I noticed, out of the corner of my eye, another dollop of butter heading for the edge of Oily's toast. This time the butter missed his shirt front and landed in his lap, leaving a stain in the sort of place that is always embarrassing.

The situation across the street was so bizarre, so unreal, that it took both of us a minute or so to realise that the unfortunate individual sitting in the wheelchair needed help. However, before either of us could get to our feet a woman in her late twenties appeared on the other side of the door, inside the building, and started gesticulating to the man in the wheelchair. She was, it seemed, telling him to let go of the handle so that she could open the door and let him in. He, however, was unwilling to let go of the handle because he knew that if he did he would roll back down the ramp, onto the pavement and probably straight into the road.

So there they both stayed. She on the inside, unable to get out, he on the outside, unable to get in.

'Damn!' said Oily suddenly, looking down and seeing the growing stains on his shirt and trousers. He hurriedly put the now cold remains of his toast down on his plate, picked up a shiny paper napkin and dabbed unsuccessfully at the buttery stains.

When I turned back to the window I was delighted to see that they seemed to be making some progress. She was pushing, gently and gingerly, on the door and he, holding onto the door handle, was rolling gently back down the slope. Eventually the door was open far enough to let the girl wriggle out. She bent down, got underneath the man's arm and then stood up at the top of the ramp between the wheelchair and the door. He was still holding onto the door handle.

119

They'd made some progress but they still hadn't solved the problem. The man in the wheelchair still couldn't get into the building and the woman who had come to his assistance couldn't get back into the building or past him down the ramp.

For all I know they're both still there, trapped together for eternity. While struggling to clean the stain off his trousers Oily caught sight of his watch and excitedly reminded me that it was well past the time we'd promised to pick up Norman. We paid our bill, hurried down the stairs and jogged back towards the hairdressing salon.

To our astonishment Norman was waiting for us outside on the pavement. He had a large bandage wrapped around his head and a red stain seeping through suggested that it wasn't just there to keep his head warm. Slumped on the pavement, with his back resting against a stretch of graffiti marked wall he looked lonely and dispirited.

Norman told us what had happened as we made our way back to the hotel.

He had, he was told as we left the salon, been given an appointment with a Ms Judy, one of the salon's hair stylists, but before she would condescend to touch his hair he would, he was informed, have to have his hair washed by one of her assistants.

Norman said he found this extremely tedious and that by the time the assistant had finished and had handed him over to Ms Judy he was suffering from a severe case of terminal boredom.

'She'd didn't seem to want to want talk about anything', said Norman miserably. 'Not even the weather!'

So, while Ms Judy tutted and hmmed her way around his scalp Norman tried to amuse himself.

'I read the labels on the shampoo bottles, counted the leaves on one of the plants and wound up my watch,' said Norman, 'and then I pulled my spectacle case out of my trouser pocket and started to polish the lenses.'

Norman said that he can't quite remember what happened next but that when he woke up he was surrounded by half a dozen very angry looking members of the staff and he could feel something warm and sticky running down the side of his face.

'It seems,' sighed Norman, 'that Ms Judy saw me polishing my spectacles under the green cloth they'd draped over me and misinterpreted the movements I was making.'

We both stared at him for a moment before realising what he meant.

'You mean . . .' began Oily, starting to chuckle.

'She thought . . .?' I added, finding it impossible not to grin.

'Exactly!' said Norman. 'She apparently hit me over the head with a shampoo bottle and called the manager. The next thing I knew I found myself waking up with a cut on the side of my head and a stain on my character.'

Oily said he thought that there was a lesson for us all in this sad story. He said that in future we should stick to old fashioned barbers who are used to cutting men's hair.

Norman said he couldn't agree more. He said that he wasn't even sure whether or not they'd actually cut his hair but that the whole sorry business had cost him ten times as much as a visit to his usual barber.

United in our feelings we hurried back to the hotel where the rest of the team was waiting for Oily to pay the bill.

*   *   *

CHAPTER SIXTEEN

When we left Newquay we headed further south west towards Tottery Poppleton, a village just outside Penzance on the south Cornish coast where we were due to play our next match the following day. Much as we love cricket I don't think any of us minded having a day's rest. Wodger was cheerful but still shaken and obviously feeling rather delicate. Norman, who had taken off his bandage, now had a patch of dried blood on his scalp in addition to a black left eye and looked very quiet and subdued. Simon's right thumb had swollen up so much that he had difficulty in holding a cricket ball. Oily's foot was badly bruised and he had acquired a definite limp. Jerry had taken his arm out of his makeshift sling but now had a huge bruise to remind him of the match at North Hawkwater. And June, who had a massive bruise on her thigh, walked rather like a cowboy who has spent too long in the saddle.

Since Wodger said he had worked out a quick cross country route that would take us through some of the county's most beautiful scenery we all followed his lead as we left the hospital.

Just over an hour later we drove back into the centre of Newquay and Wodger stopped his car and told us, with sincere apologies, that he seemed to have got a little lost.

Oily said he wasn't surprised. He said that in his experience short cuts were never anything of the sort and that as a general rule if he stopped to ask directions and someone told him of a short cut he would drive off in exactly the opposite direction.

Wodger said that it was merely a temporary problem and

that he'd soon get us down to Penzance if only we'd show a little patience. So, after a few moans from Oily, we all got back into our cars and Wodger led our small convoy out of Newquay once more.

Forty minutes later Wodger slowed to a stop on a narrow country road, climbed out of his car and, looking rather embarrassed, walked back to explain to us that we were lost again.

'Where are we now?' asked Oily, clearly running out of patience. He took his diary out of his jacket pocket and opened it to the map of England on the back page. He thrust the diary through the car window at Wodger and asked him to show us where we'd stopped.

'That's the pwoblem,' said Wodger, apologetically. 'I'm afraid I don't know where we are. There don't seem to be any signs.' Miserably he waved an arm around him to attract our attention to the total lack of signposts.

'I used to be a boy scout,' said Simon, rather diffidently, from the back seat.

Oily and I turned round to look at him.

'Moss always grows on the north side of a tree,' he said, blushing vividly. 'At least I'm pretty sure it does.' He paused and swallowed noisily. 'And cows always lie down if its going to rain.' He went an even deeper red, clearly regretting his generous offer of help. 'Or is it that they lie down if it is raining?'

He coughed, folded his arms tightly across his chest and pushed himself back into the corner of the seat as though trying to disappear from view.

'We can always wait until it gets dark,' I suggested. 'Then we can navigate with the aid of the stars.'

'Isn't there something you can do with the sun?' asked Oily. 'I seem to remember that if you point the hour hand of your watch at the sun and the minute hand in the direction you want to go then if you bisect the angle the two hands make you're facing due south.'

'That's rubbish!' I said firmly. 'We wait until it goes dark and then follow the milky way down to the plough and then follow the line made by the brightest star in the constellation and that takes us straight to the north star. Once we've found the north star the rest is simple.'

'This is quite serious,' said Wodger, looking glum. 'I haven't got much petrol left. I don't suppose you've got a spare can in the boot?'

Oily shook his head. 'What about Jerry?' he asked. 'He's bound to have a can of petrol in that old crate of his.'

We got out and walked over towards Jerry's car. He hadn't got any spare petrol either. But he did have a crate of beer so we sat down on the verge and opened up the beer.

'My mum and dad got lost once on a holiday abroad,' said Norman as we argued about which way we thought we ought to go. He said that they couldn't afford a proper holiday so they'd decided to have a day out in Calais. They'd fixed up everything with their travel agents and got special cheap day return tickets on the ferry from Dover. The plan was that they'd set off at five or six in the morning and get home again just after midnight.

Neither of Norman's parents had ever been abroad before, although during the war Norman's father had worked as a ground crew mechanic on aeroplanes which had dropped bombs on all sorts of interesting and historic places in Germany, so they were extremely excited by the whole idea.

'If they'd known just how exciting it was going to be they would have probably decided to go to Bognor Regis instead,' said Norman ominously.

Their problems started when they got off the boat in Calais and wandered away in search of a small cafe where they could buy a nice cup of tea and a plate of fish and chips. Being unaccustomed to sea travel they had both suffered a little mal de mer while on the ferry but with their feet firmly planted on French cobbles their appetites had returned.

Since they hadn't really intended to move too far away from the docks they didn't have a map with them and so after walking for half an hour or so they discovered, to their horror, that they were absolutely lost. They eventually found a small cafe where they managed to order two tiny cups of strong black coffee but their inability to speak a word of French hampered their ability to ask instructions on how best to find their way back to the town centre.

With patience, determination and rapidly developing

blisters they marched on and on in search of the town, the docks and the English Channel. For a while they followed a small flock of sea gulls on the assumption that the gulls would eventually head back to the sea but then the seagulls flew out of sight.

'They thought everything was going to be all right,' said Norman, 'when they heard what they felt sure was a ship's hooter. They speeded up a bit and sang cheerful songs to keep up their spirits as they marched off in the direction from which they'd heard the hooter.'

Sadly, it wasn't a ship's hooter at all but a factory siren telling the workers that it was time to take their lunch and so Norman's weary mum and dad found themselves surrounded by hundreds of hungry French citizens all hurrying home to their crusty bread, pâté, frogs legs, onions and red wine.

By nightfall the two adventurers found themselves on the outskirts of a small town with an unpronounceable name so they spent most of the money they had with them on renting a room for the night in a small pension. Sadly, the proprietor must have still nursed a hatred of the English left over from the Napoleonic Wars for when, next morning, they asked him for the route back to the sea (Norman explained that they communicated with le patron by miming a rowing boat, a lookout and someone being sea sick) he sent them along the main road to Paris.

At lunchtime Norman's weary parents met an English speaking gendarme who listened with some interest and considerable sympathy to their sad story.

The gendarme put Norman's parents into his car and took them along to the nearest railway station where the man in the ticket office apologised for the fact that the trains to Calais were being diverted because of essential engineering works and suggested instead that they buy tickets to Paris from which point they would be in a much better position to find their way back to the coast.

The two unhappy wanderers got to Paris without any further difficulty and bought their tickets to Calais with their few remaining francs. Unfortunately, however, all the worry and the travelling had made them tired and careless and they

125

got onto the night sleeper to Milan instead and woke up some twelve hours later in Italy. This proved to be quite a problem for an officious customs officer got very excited when they tried to get back into France. He said that without passports they would have to stay in Italy until their applications for residence permits were turned down and they could be officially deported.

By this time Norman's parents had apparently given up all hope of ever seeing their home again and were trying to decide whether they should make a break for what was then known as the Iron Curtain and seek political asylum in Yugoslavia, Rumania or one of those difficult to spell countries or try to escape into Switzerland in the hope of appealing to the United Nations when they saw a train that was filled with scores of noisy and excited English school children all heading for home.

The Italian customs officer had told Norman's parents to stay where they were while he went off to get help but they figured that there wasn't much else that could go wrong and so they took what remained of their courage in both hands and both feet and clambered aboard the train.

This was the best move they'd made since they'd left home. As they'd guessed the train was heading back for the Northern French coast and the school-children were heading for England. Their really lucky break came in the fact that there were at least three separate school parties on the train and none of the children – and none of the teachers – really knew who was or who wasn't with which particular party.

Norman's parents stayed with the train and its young cargo and succeeded in dealing with ticket collectors, customs officials and other potential hazards by simply picking out a child at random every time any sort of official approached and shouting at it very loudly and very angrily. The unfortunate child, being a child on holiday, would always be guilty of something and would look suitably apologetic and contrite while the official hurried to get past the embarrassing obstruction.

When they got back to Calais Norman's parents stood in the middle of a seething mass of by now even smellier, even noisier children and simply looked tired and overwrought.

Each genuine school teacher thought they belonged to some other school party and so no one gave the game away. By means of this simple technique, says Norman, they managed to get back to Dover some three and a half days after their return rail ticket home had expired.

We had listened to Norman's tale in silence. Enjoyed in the warmth of a comfortable pub such tales are amusing and entertaining. But when you're lost in the middle of Cornwall the whole sorry saga takes on a different character.

Eventually, the beer gone, we decided that we had little option but to continue the way we were going in the hope that we would eventually find a signpost, a village and a petrol station or, ideally, a signpost and a petrol station in a village.

Twenty minutes later we drove back into Newquay, a resort which we were getting to know quite well.

It was half past seven that evening when we eventually arrived at The Dog and Flute public house in Tottery Poppleton where Wodger had booked us all rooms. We had spent virtually the whole of our rest day sitting in motor cars driving round Cornwall.

* * *

My room at The Dog and Flute faced South East and I was woken early the following morning by the bright morning sun shining in through a gap in the curtains. I got up to adjust the curtains, intending to shut out the interfering rays of sunshine, but the view through the gap took my breath away and I could not resist the temptation to pull the curtains wider apart in order to get a better look.

Tottery Poppleton is a tiny village situated on the west side of Mount's Bay half way in between Penzance, the most Westerly of all Cornish towns, and the poetically named village of Mousehole which must surely be one of the most picturesque of all pretty Cornish villages.

By the time we'd booked into the pub and had our evening meal (a delicious fish pie served with a mountain range of fresh vegetables) it was dark and when I eventually fell into bed I was far too tired to bother looking out of my window.

But I stood there in my pyjamas and simply stared at the view, open mouthed with wonder.

127

The village itself hangs onto the edge of towering Cornish cliffs; a steep, narrow road being the only route down to the tiny, natural harbour several hundred feet below. There are three pubs in the village but The Dog and Flute is the biggest and has by far the most spectacular position.

The south east wall of the pub is no more than ten feet from the edge of an almost sheer cliff face that drops straight down to the crashing seas below. From my room I could see the harbour, filled with two dozen tiny fishing boats, all dancing on the incoming tide, the coastline as far as Penzance and, in the hazy distance, the faint outline of the easterly cliffs of Mount's Bay.

Directly underneath my window some brave gardener had planted a huge variety of summer flowers which, I discovered when I opened the window, smelt as magnificent as they looked. Half a dozen seagulls strutted about on the thin moss and grass covered rock at the very edge of the cliff.

I've heard people say that it's possible to tire of any pleasure and that daily repetition makes any joy dull and routine. But I doubt if any human with a heart or a soul could ever take that view for granted. If I had not had responsibilities to attend to back home I would have found myself a job nearby and booked myself into that room for life.

The view from the dining room, where we all joined up for breakfast, was almost equally impressive. Bright flowers, blue sea, toy fishing boats and bright blue skies turned each window into an individual masterpiece.

I sat down at a table occupied by Oily, Sharon and Simon, ordered black coffee, a full English breakfast and a freshly toasted loaf.

'Isn't this wonderful?' I said to no one in particular, leaning back in my chair with my hands behind my head and enjoying the views, the smells, and being with friends and anticipating a splendid breakfast and another wonderful day.

Oily and Simon were both busily munching their way through enormous portions of bacon, sausage and eggs but I noticed that Sharon wasn't eating at all. I looked at her and noticed that a tear had escaped from her left eye and was beginning to edge its way, rather timidly, down her left cheek.

I looked at Oily. He was too engrossed with a sausage to notice. 'What's the matter?' I asked her quietly, after a moment's hesitation.

Sharon looked at me and smiled. She looked embarrassed rather than depressed. 'I'm a bit homesick,' she said.

Simon, who was sitting between us, put down his knife and fork and looked up at her. She smiled at him. He blushed. 'Why don't you write?' he asked her. 'I do whenever I feel homesick.' He gulped. 'It always helps,' he assured her.

Sharon pulled out a paper tissue and wiped her eyes. 'I wouldn't know what to say,' she said.

'Just tell them what you've been doing,' said Simon.

Sharon laughed then, realising that Simon might think she was being rude, put her hand in front of her mouth. The half stifled laugh turned into a giggle.

'OK!' she said suddenly. Then she frowned. 'Do you know where I can get some writing paper from?' she asked him. 'And stamps?'

'I've got plenty,' Simon told her. 'Do you want me to go and get some for you?'

'When you've finished your breakfast,' said Sharon.

Simon looked down at his almost empty plate. 'I've finished,' he said.

'If I come with you will you help me with what to write?' Sharon asked him.

Simon turned even redder and looked at Oily who grinned at him.

'Watch her!' said Oily. 'It's your fountain pen she's after!'

Sharon nudged Oily with her elbow then stood up, took Simon by the hand and pulled him away from the table. 'We'll see you in a few minutes,' she said over her shoulder.

Oily watched them go then cut off a slice of sausage and nodded in their direction. 'They make a nice couple,' he said, popping the piece of sausage into his mouth.

*   *   *

At around 11.30 that morning we all gathered in the 'snug' at The Dog and Flute (the word 'snug' is not only far more romantic and evocative than such cold and empty phrases as 'lounge bar' but it also summed up the character of the room very precisely) and prepared to leave for the Tottery Poppleton XI cricket ground, reputedly the flattest piece of ground on that particular stretch of coast.

Our match was due to start at noon instead of the more normal 2.00pm and Wodger had already explained to us that the aim was to allow us to have 55 overs a side. Most of our matches are, through time constraints, restricted to a maximum of 40 overs and we approached this longer confrontation with some misgivings. Wodger tried to encourage us by pointing out that we would have not one but two intervals for rest and refreshments.

Although the cricket ground was no more than a quarter of a mile from the pub we took our cars. A few of us had been prepared to walk but Arthur had defiantly refused to contemplate such unnecessary physical activity. When he reminded us that we would have to walk back again – carrying all our equipment – after a long day's cricket we all decided that he was right.

It was a glorious morning and the views from the Tottery Poppleton ground were stupendous. The cricket pitch was situated in a former field slightly higher than The Dog and Flute and from the tiny wooden pavilion we had a similar but slightly broader view of the bay than from the pub. Actually, although I call it a pavilion it was in reality little more than a wooden garage in which was stored the team's mower and roller. There were no real dressing room facilities and so we while June and Sharon got changed in Oily's Jaguar the rest of us put on our whites behind the pavilion.

Twelve o'clock came and went and still there was no sign of our opposition. We didn't mind. We lazed around on the grass, watching a few, fluffy white clouds move effortlessly across the clear blue summer skies. Simon made a daisy chain and gave it to Sharon. June and the vicar went for a walk. Arthur began the day's serious assault on his drinking flask. Wodger, using a pencil stub and the back of his car manual, tried to work out a bowling schedule for 55 overs. Brian, who'd discovered that his broken tooth enabled him to produce an exceptionally piercing whistle practised whistling unidentifiable pop ballards.

At twelve fifteen a puffing, red faced cyclist pedalled through the gate onto the ground, dismounted and rested his bicycle against the side of the pavilion. He stood for a moment, with his hands on his hips, gasping for breath.

'The lifeboat's been called out!' he announced eventually.

We turned, automatically, and looked down in the direction of the harbour. We could see the usual variety of small boats but from such a distance it was impossible to identify any particular types of boat.

'Sinking ship?' asked Wodger.

The cyclist shook his head and beads of perspiration flew from his forehead. 'Holidaymaker on an airbed,' he told us. 'Swept out to sea.'

'That's tewible!' said Wodger.

'Happens all the time.' The cyclist took out a large, grubby handkerchief and mopped his face. 'Three times last week.'

'It was vewy good of you to cycle all this way to tell us,' said Wodger. 'But . . .'

'Oh, sorry,' the cyclist apologised. 'I should have explained.' He finished the mopping up process and stuffed the now sodden handkerchief back into his trouser pocket. 'I'm a member of the cricket club – honorary vice-president – eight of the team are in the lifeboat crew.' He shrugged unhappily. 'I'm sorry,' he said again.

'Oh that's OK,' said Wodger. 'We understand. Priorities'. He stared down at the sea again as though still looking for the lifeboat. 'I don't suppose you have any idea when they'll be back?'

The cyclist shook his head. 'It'll be late this afternoon. When they get back in they have to get the lifeboat back up the ramp, clean all the equipment and so on . . .' he took the handkerchief out again and mopped up another flood of sweat.

'So the match is pwetty much off then?' said Wodger.

'Well it is,' said the cyclist, 'but it isn't necessarily.' He unbuttoned his shirt cuffs and rolled up his sleeves. Both forearms were decorated with tattoos. 'The lifeboat here is manned by men from our village and from Trevishoe,' he explained. 'And the Trevishoe team also had a match this afternoon.'

'Which they won't be able to play?' said Wodger, catching on quickly.

'That's it!' nodded the cyclist. 'They were due to play a team that's come down from London – bankers or such like I believe.'

'So there are two teams without a match!' said Wodger.

'If you'd like to play one another you're welcome to use the ground here,' said the cyclist. 'It's the least we can do.'

Wodger looked around. We murmured, nodded and generally indicated that this seemed a good idea and a generous offer on the part of the Tottery Poppleton club.

'That's vewy kind of you,' said Wodger. 'Vewy kind indeed. How do we get in touch with this team from London?'

'Leave that to me,' said the cyclist. He climbed aboard his elderly, rust laden machine. 'I'll get a message to them,' he assured us. 'Don't you worry!' he called as he pedalled away.

*   *   *

CHAPTER SEVENTEEN

We went back to the pub for lunch and left a note pinned to the Tottery Poppleton pavilion telling our opponents where we were. Since we had no idea when they'd arrive there didn't seem much point in hanging around indefinitely in the middle of an isolated field with nowhere to sit, nothing to eat or drink and no essential facilities.

An hour later after feasting on home made bread, a surprising variety of excellent cheeses and the best collection of home made pickles I've ever seen we were ready for anything. Or at least we thought we were.

We were sitting around on wooden benches in the pub garden, sipping full bodied pints of locally brewed Cornish beer, when our opponents arrived.

I think we'd all half expected them to turn up in a convoy of BMWs, Porsches and Ferraris. But they didn't. They came on the most luxurious coach I've ever seen. It was equipped with its own kitchen, shower and toilet and had a huge video screen and a bar as well. The driver sat in a small cabin so that he would not be distracted by anything going on in the body of the vehicle.

I don't really know what any of us had expected but, although they were all employees of a London bank, they all seemed pleasant enough fellows. We introduced ourselves, shook hands and bought them all beers. Then we all climbed onto their coach for the short drive up to the Tottery Poppleton cricket ground. Since Simon was the only one of us sober enough to drive – and he doesn't have a driving licence – this seemed a sensible precaution.

The pavilion was still locked, of course. None of us had

thought to ask the red faced cyclist if he had a key. But it didn't matter much. The driver of the bankers' coach parked his vehicle next to the pavilion and our opponents got changed inside it.

When they were ready we all marched out to inspect the wicket.

That was when we realised that we didn't have any stumps or bails. We had bats, pads and all the other essential personal paraphenalia needed for a cricket match. Our opponents even had a supply of balls. But we didn't have a single cricket stump.

It was Jerry, who always carries a full set of carpenters tools in the back of his car, who solved that problem. With Brian's help he found two or three fairly straight branches and within ten minutes had produced a perfectly useable set of stumps and bails. Indeed, it was only with some difficulty that we managed to dissuade Jerry from driving down into the village to try and buy varnish with which to finish off the job properly.

The bankers' captain, a tall distinguished looking fellow called Henry, then invited Wodger out onto the pitch so that they could toss to determine the order of play. Wodger lost the toss, of course, and the bankers' captain asked Wodger if he would mind batting first. Wodger, rather more accustomed to being simply told 'You're batting!' misunderstood Henry's polite manner and said that he didn't really mind batting first but that given the choice he'd rather field. Henry said that he understood Wodger's feelings but that since he didn't have the choice it was destined to be an academic discussion and would we like to nominate an umpire.

This was our second problem.

It turned out that the bankers travelled with their own umpire and their own scorer. When Wodger pointed out that there were only eleven of us and that if we provided an umpire it would have to be one of our players Henry looked rather put out.

'I suppose that will have to do,' he said, rather condescendingly. 'If that's all you can manage.'

Wodger seemed quite upset but Oily offered to umpire until it was his turn to bat and Wodger went off to put his pads on and find Jerry who'd been promoted to open the innings with him (Norman had decided he liked a chance to see how things were shaping up before he went out to bat).

Our innings opened in an unusually optimistic mood. Oily put his dark flannels back on and allowed his white shirt to hang outside them so it looked a little like a short white coat and went out to umpire with Norman's straw panama hat perched precariously on top of his head. Wodger and Jerry then marched out to bat with determination characterising every stride. This was, we all knew, our first chance to match ourselves against another touring side, our first chance to compare ourselves with the sort of opposition our West Country opponents would meet on the summer circuit. The rest of us gathered in a huddle in the shade of the bankers coach to watch the match.

'Jerry is looking on form today,' said the vicar, lowering his binoculars.

'That was a pretty ominous looking forward defensive prod,' agreed Norman, without an ounce of sarcasm in his voice. 'Jerry's obviously intending to make a big score today.'

'I don't think I've ever seen Wodger looking quite so determined,' said Brian, who'd lost a little bit more off his broken tooth and whose every word was now accompanied by a faint whistling sound.

It was this which confused me for a moment.

But then, when Brian stopped speaking, I heard the sound much more clearly. It seemed improbable but the sound was distinctive and unmistakeable.

'Can anyone else hear a telephone ringing?' I asked.

'I was just thinking I could hear a telephone,' June said.

'It is!' said Simon. 'It's a telephone. Look!' He pointed in the direction of mid-off who, as we watched, pulled a portable telephone out of his back pocket and proceeded to talk into it.

'I've never seen anything like it!' said the vicar, clearly shocked.

The fielder seemed to be having a fairly animated conversation with someone and was now waving his free arm about. None of the other members of his team seemed in the slightest bit surprised though Wodger, Jerry and Oily were all standing and staring at him.

Eventually, a couple of minutes later, mid-off slammed the aerial back into the body of his telephone and stuffed the instrument back into his trouser pocket.

'Well, I never!' said the vicar. I've never heard anyone say: 'Well, I never!' before and had always assumed it was the sort of thing people only said in books and plays.

During the next thirty minutes or so we discovered that every player in Henry's team had a portable telephone with him. At least once an over one of the telephones would ring and the fielder would have a short conversation with the caller. Several times two or more fielders gathered together, clearly discussing the contents of a particular call. On one occasion a bowler stopped in the middle of his run up to answer a telephone call.

Despite all these interruptions (and it can't be easy to carry on batting when you hear the wicket keeper behind you answering a telephone call) Wodger and Jerry maintained their concentration magnificently. After an hour and a half we still hadn't lost a wicket but had fifty runs on the board.

Then, as though acting in response to some prearranged but invisible signal the fielding side all sat down on the grass. Wodger, Jerry and Oily were clearly totally confused by this. The reason for the sit down became clear a moment later when the driver emerged from the coach with a large tray of assorted cold drinks which he carefully offered to fielders, umpires and batsmen.

While the players were taking drinks the bankers' wicket keeper ran over towards us, climbed up into the coach and then emerged a moment or two later carrying a fax message which he had clearly been waiting for. Thoughtfully studying the fax he ran back out on the pitch again.

This was, apparently, all too much for Wodger who put down his bat and wandered across to where Henry, our opponents' captain, was deep in conversation with two members of his side, one of whom was engrossed in an agitated telephone conversation.

I was curious too. I'd never seen a cricket match interrupted so much. I couldn't help wondering whether the bankers carried their telephones out to the crease when they were batting. Tentatively, I tiptoed onto the outfield so that I could find out what was going on. The rest of the team followed me.

'I do apologise,' said Henry who looked distraught. He seemed to have aged twenty years since our innings had begun. I knew that Wodger and Jerry had made a good start but it didn't seem the sort of start to age an opponent. 'There's a bit of a crisis with the yen,' he explained.

Wodger looked as puzzled as I'm sure the rest of us felt. 'The yen?'

'The Japanese Government has apparently been up to some hanky panky – or rather one or two prominent members of the Government have,' said Henry. 'The yen's taken a battering on the foreign exchange markets and we're over exposed. We took a short position on dollars and bought puts on the index.'

The vicar looked at me with a frown on his face. I looked at him. Wodger looked at Henry. We all looked at one another. The only one of us who knew what Henry was talking about was Henry. As far as we were concerned he might as well have been talking in a foreign language.

'We have, er, something of a crisis on our hands,' explained Henry.

'Do you want to abandon the match?' Wodger asked him.

'Good heavens, no!' said Henry. 'Not if you don't mind us just making a few calls occasionally. We're trying to get out of our position and it might take us a little time.'

'I can see that,' said Wodger who clearly didn't have the faintest idea what was going on. He looked across at us and rolled his eyes skywards, then he turned and slowly walked back to his bat.

Two overs later Jerry stepped down the wicket and hit a ball from one of the bankers front line bowlers straight back over his head. Normally Jerry would have expected the ball to clear the boundary by twenty yards but he didn't hit it quite cleanly and it was clear that long-on wasn't even going to have to move to take a fairly simple catch.

Long-on had his eyes fixed firmly on the ball and his hands clasped ready to catch the ball when his telephone rang.

You couldn't help but feel sorry for the fellow. You could

see the agony in his eyes as he tried to decide what to do. For an instant everyone else on the field froze. Then mid-on and long-off both started to sprint towards him as fast as they could.

Frantically, long-on pulled out his telephone, extended the aerial with a practised flourish and pressed a button or two. He listened for a moment, shouted: 'Wait!' and then turned his face upwards to try and get a sight on the ball again. He tucked the telephone between his right ear and his right shoulder so that he could cup his hands ready to take the catch.

Then he noticed that mid-on, puffing and wheezing, was no more than ten yards away from him and bearing down upon him like a runaway train.

'I'll take it!' He shouted. 'Mine! Mine!'

Mid-on skidded to a halt but distracted long-on. The result was that the ball hit long-on straight in the mouth. He fell backwards onto the ground and his telephone bounced harmlessly on the grass.

Horrified, we stared at him. We watched as he slowly raised himself onto one elbow and you could feel the relief around the ground. We all thought that he must have been killed. Slowly, as he sat up, we all realised that the ball, which seemed firmly stuck in his mouth, was still in play.

'I've never seen anyone caught by a fielder's mouth before,' said Oily.

He wasn't the only one for whom this was a new experience.

Wodger said he wondered if a catch taken in a fielder's mouth was entirely legal.

Henry, the bankers captain, said he rather thought it was. And then, as mid-on and long-off helped pull the ball out of long-on's mouth he looked a little worried. He bent forwards to examine the ball more carefully. We all moved closer to do the same.

Half a dozen of long-on's teeth were still embedded in it.

'Are those your own teeth, Nigel?' The captain asked his fielder.

Nigel put a finger into his mouth and removed the shattered remains of a set of false teeth. He shook his head. Not surprisingly, he still looked dazed.

'Oh dear!' said Henry. He turned to Oily. 'How good are you on Law 32?'

Oily's puzzled look answered the question adequately.

'As I remember it,' said Henry, 'the Law states that a catch shall be considered to have been fairly made if the ball lodges in a fielder's clothes or in the wicket keepers pads.' He took a fragment of broken denture from long-on's hand and examined it. 'Now the question is,' he continued, 'do you think a fellow's false teeth can be reasonably considered to be classified as clothing?'

'Ith parth oth my bothy!' protested long-on almost incoherently. Without his teeth his face had taken on a strange look and his mouth had almost disappeared. A trickle of blood from an area of damaged gum appeared at a corner of his mouth.

'Well, not really, old chap!' Henry insisted, rather sadly. 'They're false teeth aren't they? Not the same thing at all.'

'Buth ith I hath a falth arm ith would be parth oth my bothy!' argued long-on miserably.

'That's true!' agreed Henry, with a nod. 'We'll have to leave it to the umpires.' He turned away to talk to his own team's umpire who was standing next to Oily listening to this bizarre conversation.

Sadly, long-on put the remains of his dentures into his trouser pocket and bent to pick up his portable telephone which was still lying on the grass.

'Hello?' he said, holding the telephone to his ear. 'Oh, hello! You're thill there!'

He listened for a few moments and as he listened his face gradually grew paler and paler.

'No!' He shouted. 'No! No! No! I wath noth thalking thoo you!' He was now as pale as his shirt. 'Malcolm? Malcolm? Are you thill there?'

Looking every inch a broken man long-on automatically turned off his telephone and pushed the aerial back into place. He leant forwards and tapped Henry on the shoulder.

'We're finithed!' he announced.

'Don't be so silly!' said Henry, turning round. 'We'll get the fellow out in the next over. Don't worry about it.' He started to smile at long-on but noticed how pale he'd become.

'Good heavens, Nigel!' He said. 'You look like death. Are you all right?'

'When I wath thrying to thake that catch . . .' said long-on.

'What's happened, Nigel?' shouted Henry, now looking as worried as long-on did. Attracted by the panic in Henry's voice the rest of the team hurried over.

'I shouthed tho the otherth,' sobbed long-on, 'tho thell them that the catch wath mine . . .'

'Yes, yes!' shouted Henry. 'What the hell's happened?'

'My phone wath swithed on . . .'

Henry was now getting hysterical.

'Malcolm from the Thitty Bank wath calling . . .'

'What did he want?' screamed Henry, taking hold of long-on's shirt front and shaking him. 'What have you done?'

'He wanthed tho thell me thome yen,' said long-on, with tears now streaming down his cheeks.

Henry let go of long-on's shirt and stepped backwards. Everyone in their side was now silent and hanging on long-on's next words.

'I theem tho have bought three hundred million pounths worth . . .'

Long-on fell onto his knees and pounded the grass with his portable telephone. 'Ith wathn't my fault!' He sobbed. 'Ith wathn't!'

'I say,' said Oily gently but reprovingly, 'do be careful! You're damaging the outfield with your telephone.'

After that things rather fell apart.

Once he'd got over the immediate shock of what Nigel had inadvertently done Henry valiantly offered to carry on. But it was obvious that his heart wasn't really in it.

And who could blame him?

After an agonising twenty minutes, during which every member of the team of bankers must have telephoned every bank and broking firm in London, Henry announced that his bank had gone bust.

None of us knew what to say.

What *do* you say to a group of men who have just seen their highly paid jobs, bonuses, incentive schemes, company cars, pension plans and myriad miscellaneous perks disappear?

Eventually, Wodger called us all back onto the field and suggested to Henry that we call it a day.

As he watched Wodger and Jerry (the umpires had jointly decided that the catch had not been fairly held) walk off the field, accompanied by the entire fielding side, Arthur, lifted himself up onto one elbow and spoke to me.

'What's up?' He demanded. He looked up at the bright blue sky and frowned. 'Why are they coming off?' he asked. 'The light seems good enough to me.'

* * *

CHAPTER EIGHTEEN

At around half past five that evening the peace and quiet of The Dog and Flute was shattered by the arrival of a television film crew.

After the premature end of our match against the touring bankers we had made our own way back to the pub and left them preparing for the long journey back to London. We'd invited them to share a few drinks and a meal with us before their departure but, not surprisingly I suppose, they'd declined. In the immortal words of Greta Garbo they 'wanted to be alone'.

'We were obviously destined not to play a match today,' said the vicar, lounging back in an ancient wood framed canvas deck-chair. 'One should never fight against one's destiny.' He lay back, closed his eyes and gave every impression of a man destined for sleep.

I took a sip from the pint of local brew that Jerry had just bought me and wiped the froth off my upper lip. 'Where's Sharon?' I asked Oily, looking around and noticing her absence.

'She's gone for a walk with Simon,' Oily replied, with a smile, 'they both wanted to see the harbour.'

'They seem to be getting on well together,' I commented.

Oily picked up his glass of gin and tonic (quite a lot of gin and hardly any tonic) and shook it so that the ice cubes rattled against the sides of the glass. 'They're good for each other,' he said.

I looked at him and raised an eyebrow. 'She's a bit young for me to be honest,' Oily confided. 'Wants to talk about pop groups I've never heard of and is desperate to find true love.'

I nodded, understanding, and took another sip of my beer. It was very good beer.

It was then that the television film crew arrived.

Or, rather, it was then that we first became aware of their presence.

'That was really super!' cried a strange voice.

We looked up.

A fat, rather sweaty little man in a pair of very scruffy, oil stained jeans and a grey polo neck sweater that had an undecipherable slogan on the front and ancient sweat stains under the arms came up to us grinning inanely.

'That was really super,' he repeated, breathing stale cigar smoke over us. 'But I wonder if you could do it just once more and keep a little closer together this time.'

Oily and I looked at one another and then looked at the small fat man. Then we looked beyond him and noticed that he was accompanied by a man with a camera, a man with a tape recorder and a microphone and a male model. It wasn't immediately apparent whether or not the male model was alive.

'It'll make a perfectly lovely opening shot,' said the fat little man. He clasped his hands together in front of his chest as though in prayer. He looked an unlikely supplicant.

Another man, dressed like the others in dirty blue jeans and a dark, stained sweater came up to one side of us and held a battery operated lamp above our heads.

Oily looked up and scowled at the man. 'Do you mind?' he said sharply. 'The heat from your damned lamp is melting my ice.'

The man who was holding the light ignored Oily completely. A youth of indeterminate sex struggled into view carrying two large canvas hold-alls. The male model proved that he was, indeed, alive by taking a small mirror out of his blazer pocket and checking his necktie, teeth and hair. On discovering that all these items were in position he slid the mirror back into his pocket and looked around furtively to see if anyone had noticed. When he saw me looking at him he turned on his smile. It looked about as genuine as a seventy pence piece.

He moved a couple of paces closer and held out his hand. I looked at it as though he was offering to sell it to me. The skin was perfectly white and unblemished. The nails were clean and neatly trimmed. He wore a large gold ring on the little finger of his left hand.

'Hello!' he said, broadening the smile. I'm prepared to swear that his eyelashes fluttered. He introduced himself and spoke as though we ought to know who he was. He said it gently as though not wanting to give us too much joy in one brief instant. He said it quietly as though convinced that the introduction was unnecessary.

'Tell this moron to move his bloody light,' said Oily. 'He's melting my bloody ice.'

'I'm so sorry,' apologised the male model. He fluttered a few finger tips and the man with the light backed away out of range. I couldn't get over how much the speaker reminded me of one of those plastic models that stand in the windows of gents outfitters. He wore a blue blazer with well polished brass buttons (all of which were fastened!), a pair of dark blue slacks with razor sharp creases down the front, a pair of black Gucci loafers with decorative brass buckles, a pale blue shirt and an immaculately knotted blue and maroon spotted tie. His hair was cut short in that strange style television interviewers favour so that it somehow remains unruffled whatever the wind may do. His teeth were white, sparkling and expensively capped and the smile was still as fixed, precise and meaningless as it has been when he'd first switched it on. His eyes were bright blue and quite dead. There didn't seem to be anything behind them.

'I'm so sorry to bother you,' he lied. He looked at each of us in turn and extended his frail looking hand another few inches. Feeling embarrassed I reached out and attempted to shake hands. But he moved his fingers back as my hand reached his and I was left clutching a clump of damp flesh.

'I'm from the local television station,' he explained.

'Gosh!' said Oily, feigning surprise.

'I thought you might not have realised,' said the male model. He did not seem blessed with a powerful sense of humour. 'We've been asked by the national television news programme to produce a short film about the team from the London bank that's just gone under.'

We stared at him in silence.

Brian, who'd been sitting some distance away from us, got up and headed for the bar, carrying his empty beer glass with him. He paused as he passed us. 'Do you want a refill?' Then he looked at the male model and his companions. 'Who are these pillocks?' he asked.

Both Oily and I said that we were fine for the moment and I explained that the pillocks were from the local television company. Brian sniffed disdainfully and disappeared into the bar.

'Could we ask you a few questions?' asked the male model. 'I believe you played a game of cricket against them this afternoon?'

'No and yes,' said Oily bluntly.

'I beg your pardon?' The male model looked confused.

"No' you can't ask us a few questions and 'yes' we played a game of cricket against them this afternoon.'

'I don't think you understand,' said the male model. 'This is for the national news.' He put a lot of emphasis on the word 'national'. It was clearly important to him.

'Why don't you speak to the bankers?' asked Oily.

'Unfortunately, they'd gone by the time we'd arrived,' said the male model. 'You're all we've got.'

'Then you've got a problem,' said Oily.

'This is an important story,' said the male model. He was flushed now and beginning to look agitated. 'It's an opportunity for you to state your side of the story.'

'Super,' said Oily drily. He would have probably sounded more thrilled if someone had told him that he had just acquired herpes.

'There's really no need to be shy,' the male model assured us. He was now beginning to sweat.

'Bugger off!' said Oily quietly.

The television interviewer seemed startled by this. He drew himself up to his full five foot seven inches and swallowed. Sweat was now dripping off his nose and chin. He turned round and looked at the small fat man who was frowning. The cameraman had put his camera down and was squatting on the floor lighting a cigarette.

Brian, returning from the bar, pushed past, carrying several drinks on a round metal tray and returned to his seat. He handed the drinks to Norman, Jerry and Wodger. Arthur was still drinking from his flask.

'Why don't you go and interview the lifeboat crew?' asked Oily. 'They've been out saving lives this afternoon.'

'Don't be silly!' snapped the male model. He took a large, neatly folded linen handkerchief out of his trouser pocket and dabbed at the sweat on his forehead, nose and chin without unfolding the handkerchief. He put the handkerchief away in his trouser pocket. He and the small fat man moved closer together and whispered furiously to one another.

'I'll pay you £25 and not a penny more,' said the male model, turning back to face us.

Oily said nothing but reached into his trouser pocket. He took out a fistful of crumpled notes and carefully picked out five ten pound notes.

'If I give you £50,' he said, offering the notes to the male model, 'will you piss off and play somewhere else with your friends?'

In the background the cameraman sniggered.

The male model changed colour faster than a traffic light. Bright red he opened his mouth to speak but nothing came out of it. Furious, he tossed his head, turned on his heel and left. We didn't see him or his crew again.

'I hate bloody television people,' said Oily. 'Always so full of their own self importance.'

'I gathered you didn't like them,' I admitted.

'I nearly appeared on television once,' said Oily.

I sipped at my beer and waited for him to continue.

He said he'd been invited to a studio where they were recording a programme in which two teams of Scandanavian potters were due to argue about the influence of lesbianism on seventeenth century Spanish pottery. He said he was only invited because a friend of a friend knew one of the researchers and they were absolutely desperate for people to make up an audience and clap at all the right moments.

Oily said, however, that as the minutes ticked away and the floor manager kept marching about shouting instructions he got more and more nervous. Eventually he could bear it no longer. His need to obey nature overcame all other considerations and he rushed out of the studio and into the nearest men's lavatory.

What Oily didn't know when he sat down was that five minutes earlier a researcher from one of the television company's nature study programmes, given the task of disposing of a jar of leeches which had been starring in a programme about river wild life, had deposited the now hungry but unwanted starlets into the very same lavatory. In careless haste, and ignorant of the staying power of these small creatures, the researcher had assumed that a single flush would rid the pan of living evidence and send a jar of former performers hurtling sewer-wards where they would meet an end of some kind.

In the event, of course, the end they met was Oily's.

When Oily's plump and no doubt succulent looking cheeks settled above them the leeches abandoned their hold on the ice like sides of the lavatory pan and headed heavenwards.

When leeches attach themselves to human skin they do so silently and without pain and so when Oily stood up a few minutes later he was aware only of a sense of relief. He was certainly not aware of the small school of dependents which had become attached to his person.

It was only when he was about to button up his fly that he noticed that his previously pink and flaccid member had acquired a turgor and a colour that seemed unusual to say the least. When, on closer examination, Oily discovered that what he could see was in fact a leech starting its breakfast he did what most men would have done under similar circumstances. He panicked.

Instead of calmly fastening his fly, walking to the studio canteen, collecting a salt cellar, returning to the privacy of the lavatory and getting rid of the leeches in the traditional, time honoured way he tore at the leeches in disgust and terror.

When, after managing to tear one leech from his person Oily put a hand behind him and discovered that there were at least half a dozen more still attached to various sensitive parts of his nether regions he lost all touch with common sense. Terrified, he tore off his trousers and his underpants and threw them onto the floor. And, with blood pouring from

147

a number of tiny skin punctures, he ran out into the corridor.

By this time it is fair to say that Oily was not thinking clearly.

Not knowing where else to go he ran straight back into the television studio. It probably wasn't the wisest thing he could have done.

He was ejected by two of the television company's toughest security men and observed by viewers as nothing more than a pink blur, momentarily adding colour and movement to a dull and otherwise unmemorable programme.

*   *   *

I know someone else who almost appeared on television.

Basil is an estate agent; an apparently sane and prosaic estate agent. Basil's hobby is astrology. For years he has been an avid student of the subject. He has a vast library of books on astrology and even has a computer programmed to provide astrological forecasts for his friends and neighbours. Everyone knows what they're getting for Christmas from Basil.

About eighteen months ago Basil wrote a book on the subject which was completely ignored by literary editors, critics and reviewers but which very nearly gave him his fifteen minutes of fame.

It all began, unpredictably, with a baggage handlers strike at Athens airport.

The strike meant that an eminent guest who was due to appear on one of the nation's leading television talk shows was unable to get out of Greece and into England. So, desperate to fill five minutes with something, the producer found Basil's book, telephoned him and asked him if he'd like to appear.

Would a politician like a knighthood?

Basil was desperately excited by the invitation. He knew very well that a spot on this particular television programme would instantly help his publishers sell thousands of copies of his book, turn him into a household name for a day and enable him to trade in his five year old Ford for something with a spoiler and go-faster stripes.

Determined to make sure that all his friends in the estate agency business saw him on the show he spent several hours before the programme ringing round and letting the news fall as casually as possible into the conversation.

'... well, I must go,' he'd say after about two minutes of chatter about the weather, 'I've got to rush ... I'm due to appear on television this evening ...'

He was so anxious to work his way through his address book that he quite forgot the time. He was still only half way through the list of people he wanted to call when he discovered that he had only forty minutes to get to the studio.

'You will have to rush,' said one of the friends he'd called. 'The programme's on soon isn't it? You're not ringing from home are you?'

Basil leapt into his car and shot off at a tremendous pace, leaving a trail of mechanised mayhem behind him. There was a nasty near miss with a bus, a skid around a traffic island and a collision, right outside the studios with a taxi, but he made it with several minutes to spare and ran into the television centre tremendously relieved. He even paused for a second and considered telephoning one or two additional friends from the studio foyer.

Unfortunately, it was all a waste of time for the show was cancelled.

The director himself came out to apologise. He explained that the interviewer, the star of the show, had been late arriving and had been involved in an accident while on the way into the studio.

'He isn't badly injured,' the director assured Basil. 'But he's badly shaken. Some buffoon ran into the side of his taxi.' He shrugged to convey his sadness and sympathy. 'He feels too shaken to go on with the show so we're going to run one of last year's favourite programmes and give the viewers another chance to see that.'

The director put a hand on Basil's shoulder. 'Some other time, perhaps?' he suggested, turning away and hurrying off along the corridor.

Needless to say that was the end of Basil's fifteen minutes of fame.

*　　*　　*

149

CHAPTER NINETEEN

Our next match was due to take place the following day at the cricket ground behind the Maiden's Arms in Plymouth.

We woke and got up early that morning knowing that we had quite a long drive ahead of us. Once again the sun was shining, once again the sea and sky were both so blue that the horizon was virtually invisible. The flowers outside The Dog and Flute seemed brighter and more full of fragrance than before.

The temptation to abandon the tour and stay there for ever was almost irresistible – but loyalty and common sense proved too powerful an opposition. I packed my bags after promising myself that I would return.

At breakfast Oily was alone.

'Where's Sharon?'

'Haven't seen her since last night,' answered Oily, putting a forkful of scrambled egg into his mouth. 'When she and Simon went down to look at the harbour.'

'Do you think they're all right?' I asked, worried for their safety. 'Shouldn't we have gone to look for them?'

'I said I hadn't seen her,' said Oily.

I looked at him, puzzled.

'I *heard* her!' grinned Oily. 'They're OK.'

He spiked a piece of mushroom, scooped up a forkful of tomato and added the mixture to the scrambled egg.

'Don't you mind?'

Oily swallowed and shook his head at the same time. I was impressed by his versatility.

'Don't get me wrong,' he said, 'Sharon's great company but ...' he thought for a moment and broke a piece of toast in two. He wiped one of the pieces of toast across his plate and then carefully bit a piece off it. 'She's never even *heard* of Ted Dexter!'

The two young lovers nearly missed breakfast. They entered the dining room hand in hand and Oily waved to them cheerfully, calling them over to our table.

'Sleep well?' he asked them both.

I've never seen anyone blush quite so dramatically as Simon did.

Sharon kissed Oily on the forehead and Oily put his arm round her waist in a friendly, almost paternal, sort of way.

I pushed back my chair and stood up. 'Don't be long!' I said to Sharon and Simon. 'We'll have to leave in ...', I looked at my watch, '... half an hour or so.' I looked at Oily. 'Coming?'

'Sure!' said Oily. He emptied his coffee cup and stood up. He winked at Simon who somehow managed to go even redder.

'Do you think his mother will think I've looked after him properly?' I asked Oily, as we left the dining room.

'Absolutely!' nodded Oily. 'This tour has been an educational experience for him.'

In the corridor outside the dining room we passed June. She was reading a letter.

'Not an income tax demand, I hope?' said Oily lightheartedly.

Neither of us was prepared for what happened next. Competent, capable, rational, sensible June suddenly exploded in a cascade of tears and flung her arms around Oily's neck.

Oily patted her on the back in an attempt to comfort her.

'There, there!' he said. 'Now, now!' Over her shoulder he looked at me in desperation. For once not even Oily knew what to do.

'What is it?' I asked her. 'What's the matter? Is it something in the letter?' I asked. Sherlock Holmes would have been able to learn a few things from me when it comes to understanding people.

The mention of the letter seemed to make things worse. June sobbed louder than ever.

'Come on now,' said Oily. 'Things are rarely as bad as

151

they seem …'. He patted her on the back again and then gave her a big hug.

'Who was the letter from?' I asked her.

'My husband!' sobbed June at last. She had the letter crumpled in her left hand. Without being seen I tried to read what it said but couldn't.

'Sergeant Tate?' said Oily. There was a strong element of surprise in his voice. I could understand it. Neither of us could see Sergeant Tate as a letter writer. In particular we couldn't see him as the author of letters likely to break a woman's heart.

June nodded and sniffed. I took the handkerchief out of my pocket and offered it to her. She wiped her eyes and then blew her nose.

'I'm sorry!' she said. 'I feel such a fool.'

'Don't be silly!' I said. I put what I hoped was a reassuring hand on her shoulder.

'What's the letter say?' asked Oily, who has never been one to put someone else's sense of privacy above his own sense of curiosity. I'd been prepared to try and read the letter but I wouldn't have dreamt of actually asking June what it contained.

'He's leaving me,' said June.

'Oh dear!' said Oily. He patted June on the back again. 'Never mind!' he added. It sounded as trite then as it probably looks now.

'He's joining the Hong Kong police force,' said June. 'He's leaving before I get back.'

'Crumbs!' said Oily. 'That's a bit sudden, isn't it?'

'He's leaving me the house and the car,' said June.

'Well that's good, isn't it?' asked Oily.

'Try not to be too upset,' I said. 'Maybe it's for the best?'

June pushed herself away from Oily and turned her tear stained face towards me. 'Upset?' she said. She laughed. 'I'm not upset!' she told me. 'It's the best news I've ever had!' She burst into tears again. 'I'm so happy,' she said, 'now that Kurt and I will be able to be together all the time.'

Oily, with June's arms draped around his shoulders, looked at me over her shoulder. He shrugged. I shrugged back at him.

'You're not miserable?' said Oily.

June shook her head.

'These are tears of joy?'

June nodded vigorously.

'Have you told the vicar yet?'

A shake of the head.

'Then let's find him,' said Oily, 'and tell him the good news.'

'Yes,' said June, 'that sounds nice.'

We left The Dog and Flute twenty minutes later than planned. All things considered that wasn't too bad. Sharon and Simon had difficulty in tearing themselves out of each other's arms long enough to pack and June and the vicar had a similar problem.

We left behind peace, beauty and tranquillity. We hadn't had much success with our cricket while staying in Tottery Poppleton but it had, nevertheless, been a memorable two nights.

And as we left I think we all felt more than a little sad as we realised that we had just one more match to play and then the tour would be over.

*   *   *

There are invariably two ways to travel from one place to another: the fast, direct, route to be used by lorries, commercial travellers and people in a hurry and the slow, pretty, scenic route. We were, strictly speaking, in something of a hurry since our match in Plymouth was due to start in less than four hours but, nevertheless, we chose the pretty route. There are times in a cricket team's life when caution has to be thrown to the wind.

I'm glad we did. North Cornwall may have the more rugged coastline and the wilder surf of the Atlantic but the coast of South Cornwall is pretty in a softer, gentler way. North Cornwall is tough but romantic. South Cornwall is romantic but tough.

For me, one of the great joys of travelling in Cornwall is the fact that the entire county is, on the whole, still untouched by the horrors of the twentieth century. The countryside is wild and real and the people are wild and real too. Cornwall is one of the few parts of England that has

153

not yet been ruined by the architects and the planners. The surveyors have not yet found it worth their while to ruin the county or its countryside.

Wherever you go in Cornwall (or, indeed, Devon) the towns and the villages are built on tradition and need rather than planning expediency.

There are, I'm pleased to say, no new towns in the West Country.

I went to Britain's best known new town, Milton Keynes, once and the memory haunts me still. Attracted by the posters, the advertisements, the jokes and a feeling that I ought to take a peep at the future before the future enveloped me I decided to spend a day there. It was, I recall with a shiver, a daunting, haunting, deeply depressing, nightmarish experience.

In some ways Milton Keynes is, like most new towns, a pleasant enough place. There are lots of open spaces. The roads are wide, well built and smooth. The countryside is attractive enough. The shopping precinct is impressive, spacious and comprehensive. The car parks are enormous. There are neat rows of houses, factories and public buildings and there are no traffic jams.

There is nothing repulsive about Milton Keynes and it ought, I suppose, to be a marvellous place in which to live and to work. It's a cleverly designed town and the people who built it obviously took great care when building it.

But to me Milton Keynes seemed to be no more a town than a plastic topped kitchen table is a piece of furniture or a bowl of prepackaged breakfast cereal is a meal. It is a place where people live, work and shop. But I can't honestly see anyone ever calling it 'home' with any real sense of pride.

What is wrong with it, of course, is that it is so carefully designed, so thoroughly organised, so well planned and so precise that it is deeply depressing as a place. It has, in short, no soul.

They're building new towns like this all over the world these days. All in the same dull, anonymous architectural style. All devoid of character. Milton Keynes could be a small American town, a small German town or a small Dutch town. There are no uncertainties, no surprises and no really playful or wasteful eccentricities. There is nothing to suggest that the town was designed by people. Nothing to suggest that the town will ever acquire a real personality of its own. Nothing to suggest that the town will ever be anything other than a bland, uninteresting groups of buildings put up to solve a housing shortage.

They've been doing the same thing with hotels for years now. Go anywhere in the world and you can find yourself staying in a hotel that has a standard design, standard decor and standard staff. You could be having breakfast or going to bed in Chicago, Paris or Hong Kong. You can find your way around your room blindfold. Everything is in exactly the same place. Nothing varies.

They're even doing it to existing towns these days.

Town planners are knocking down all the interesting bits. They are only interested in things that are functional. They are impatient with variations in style, texture, shape or size. They are intolerant of contradictions. They don't like seeing the results of mixed architectural marriages. They don't like the thought that building styles may have bumped into one another over the years. They don't like towns to have personal identities.

Is it surprising that sane and sensible people become vandals and graffiti writers?

The real problem with Milton Keynes is that the people who planned and built the town did too good a job. They did their job so well that they didn't leave any room for mistakes. They left no room for the errors and imperfections that are an essential part of life. Here and there you can see signs that someone has tried to inject a touch of humour or a note of human presence. But they are like footprints in the desert: lost and unnoticeable. There are no real follies. And the truth is that you cannot stick personality or warmth onto a new town any more than you can solder a soul into a robot.

The superficial symptom of this change for the worse is the fact that tomorrow's villages and towns are given such silly names.

How, for example, can anyone take pride in living in a town called Welwyn Garden City? What a strange name for a grown up place! The people who thought it up might have been pleased with themselves but they should have been satisfied with congratulating themselves and should then have thought up something more traditional, more prosaic, more real.

Welwyn Garden City is the sort of name they favour in America where they have places called Pleasantville. But it isn't a proper name for an English town. Decent, properly grown up places should either have solid, hard working, respectable names like Wolverhampton or Birmingham or Manchester, solid with honest muck and grime, sounding of factories and machines; or they should have fanciful, delicate names like Morton in the Marsh, Chipping Campden, Stow on the Wold or Mousehole. Those are all proper names for English towns.

The name Welwyn Garden City reminds me of those funny names that boxers, wrestlers and snooker players give themselves to make themselves sound more colourful. A boxer called Cedric Kipling would feel emasculated. He would know he would never attract the crowds. He'd be conscious of cheating the paying customers and he'd feel ashamed every time he heard the referee shout out his name. No one called Cedric Kipling could ever be a contender for a world championship. No, if you're a boxer you have to be called 'Boy Steamhammer Kipling' or 'Hard Hands Kipling' or even Cedric 'Iron Jaw' Kipling.

The same sort of thing is true of snooker players. A carefully chosen name can make a man a box office draw.

But towns are different and I don't think they should be demeaned in this way. A place should make up its mind whether it wants to be serious and solid (like Bradford or Liverpool) or flightly and rather whimsical (like Moles Chamber or North Radworthy). It shouldn't be made to sound comical or sad, like a breakfast cereal or a type of yoghurt.

Cornwall is safe from all this. Cornwall is full of steep, almost impassable lanes and cobbled pathways. It is full of old stone buildings and fairytale rooftops. Cornwall, like Devon, is full of real places and real people.

*   *   *

CHAPTER TWENTY

The last match of our tour was due to take place on the village green at Upton Bulkworthy, a small village just outside Plymouth.

When arranging the tour Wodger had asked each club secretary or captain to recommend a local pub, inn or small hotel where we could find good, simple, clean accommodation and plenty of good, plain food. The captain of the Upton Bulkworthy team had recommended a pub called The Maiden's Arms which, he said, overlooked the village green. The captain had, said Wodger, been full of praise for the establishment and had assured him that we would receive a warm welcome.

What Wodger didn't know was that the Upton Bulkworthy cricket captain and the landlord of The Maiden's Arms were one and the same person.

The pub was completely dedicated to the game of cricket. All the door handles were made out of bails. The bar was decorated with old cricket bats, elegantly framed copies of famous cricket prints, framed scorecards and team photographs. The seating was provided by old cricket ground benches (long since replaced with individual plastic bucket seats) which still bore their stencilled numbers. And instead of being labelled 'In' and 'Out' the doors to and from the kitchen were labelled 'Out' and 'Not Out' in the famous style of the gent's lavatories in the basement of the pavilion at Lords.

After he'd pulled us all pints of a recommended local brew the landlord, Tony Parsons, explained that when he'd bought the pub five years earlier it had been called The Crafty Ferret and that no one had played cricket on the village green since before the outbreak of the second world war.

'You won't believe it now,' he said, 'but five years ago our village green was covered in thistles, dandelions, buttercups and poppies. The locals walked their dogs on it and the ground had been churned up by kids on bicycles and tourists driving onto it in their cars to have picnics.'

We dutifully looked out of the bar window at the village green and made suitable noises of admiration. None of us mentioned but all of us noticed that there were rather a lot of daisies, buttercups and dandelions in evidence for a cricket pitch.

The landlord served us all with lunches which really were fit for ploughmen (half a small loaf each, a huge chunk of cheese, a small mound of fresh butter and a shiny red apple) and reminded us that the match was due to start in just under three quarters of an hour.

As we drank our beer and munched at our bread and cheese we watched as our opponents for the afternoon gathered in the shade of a massive oak tree.

They were a motley looking crew, as varied in age and size as we ourselves, but they clearly took their cricket seriously. Already changed for the match (there were no dressing rooms available other than the gents' lavatories at The Maiden's Arms) they had driven, cycled and walked to the ground in their whites.

As we watched, comfortably relaxed in the pub bar, they began a pre-match training regime that was clearly routine. They started with simple arm swinging exercises, moved on to a strange, hopping sort of exercise that was presumably designed to loosen up the muscles in their legs and then proceeded to an exhausting and exhaustive round of press ups, sit ups (holding onto one another's ankles) and leg raising movements.

'What's going on out there?' Oily asked the barmaid. Our landlord, the club captain, had long since excused himself from service behind the bar and joined his team out on the village green.

'Callisthenics!' replied the barmaid, a sensible, stout looking woman in her late forties. She wore a black, shapeless smock and had a large, hairy mole on her upper lip.

'What's it all for?' asked Oily, throwing a handful of peanuts down his throat with such experienced efficiency that few of them even touched his tongue or tonsils.

'Oh, Mr Parsons is very keen on winning,' replied the barmaid sternly. 'He likes the team to get properly loosened up ready for the match.'

Oily took another look out through the bar window and bit a gherkin in half. 'But it's a game!' He laughed. 'Supposed to be fun.' He sent the remaining half a gherkin to its fate and nodded a head in the direction of the village green. 'That doesn't look like fun.'

'Mr Parsons says that if a game is worth playing then it's worth winning,' said the barmaid.

Oily looked at her and said nothing. He looked at me and rolled his eyes upwards in despair.

I know some people won't agree with me about this but I'm entirely with Oily. I sometimes think the world has gone mad. These days everything seems to have been taken over by people who are always intent on learning things, bettering themselves and doing well. These days just about everything has to have a purpose and a meaning. Things have to be done properly. There isn't much room left for 'fun'.

When I first started to play golf, seven or eight years ago, the professional who taught me insisted that everything had to be taken seriously.

I learnt that you can't just toddle round the course digging up the turf, losing balls and generally enjoying the exercise, the company and the fresh air. These days you have to buy books telling you how to improve your swing, video cameras telling you where to put your feet and balls which are technically designed to give you maximum bounce and length. I learnt that real golfers worry a lot about their game and I was taught that people who just hack around having a good time are second rate citizens to be despised and held in low esteem.

The futility of all it finally dawned on me a couple of years ago. It was a good summer and I'd spent four long hours trailing around a bone hard golf course in a club tournament. I was making my way back to the changing room when the professional caught sight of me and called me over. He told

159

me that I'd developed a bit of a twitch in my swing and suggested that I went straight over to the practice green to work on it.

Well, I was absolutely knackered but I went. I hadn't enjoyed the game of golf but I knew that if I didn't go to the practice ground I'd feel guilty. I'd had a long hard week and I really wanted a rest but I felt I had to knuckle down and take the game seriously.

On the way out to the practice ground I passed a couple of lazy good for nothing layabouts who I knew. They were both sprawled in deck chairs and doing absolutely nothing apart from contribute to the profits of a large international brewery.

As I limped back from the practice ground, three quarters of an hour later, they were still there. And as I limped wearily into the changing rooms, where I knew only too well that there would be a stench of damp socks and a queue for the shower, I felt rather aggrieved. It didn't seem fair. It certainly wasn't fun. It was too hot for golf and far too hot to be hammering away at golf balls on the practice green. I love golf almost as much as I love cricket but I felt that there are times for playing sport and times for lounging in deck chairs. This seemed more like a time for lounging in a deck chair. I felt I'd been tricked by my own false sense of ambition.

I vowed there and then never to take any game too seriously.

And it's made life much more fun.

'I suppose we ought to make a move!'

The sound of Wodger's voice woke me from my daydream. Sitting on the pub's old cricket bench, with the sun streaming through the windows, I'd drifted back a few years. When Wodger spoke I'd been watching Michael Holding bowling from the Pavilion End at Lords.

'They look terribly keen,' moaned Brian, staring out of the window. 'Look at them now!'

We all turned and stared at our opposition. They were now busy waving their arms around like a squad of demented traffic policemen.

'I feel tired just watching them,' said Norman, wearily.

'They train in a gym in Plymouth every Monday and Thursday evening.'

We looked round. The barmaid, busy polishing a glass, had a smug look on her face. 'Mr Parsons says that fitness is the key to success in all walks of life.' She opened her mouth, exhaled loudly into the glass, polished it again and held it up to the window so that she could check that it sparkled properly.

'Come on,' said Oily loudly. He stood up and stretched his arms which made loud, arthritic creaks of protest. 'Let's stuff the bastards out of sight.'

We drained our glasses, went upstairs to our rooms to change into our playing kit and re-united outside the pub's front door a few minutes later.

'That shirt looks as if you haven't washed it since we started the tour!' said Wodger to Jerry.

Jerry looked down at his shirt which was covered in grass stains and muddy brown marks where he'd polished the ball on it (we hadn't played with a bright red ball for years). 'I haven't!' he said.

'That's disgusting!' said Wodger.

'How could we wash our clothes?' asked Brian. 'We haven't even seen a launderette!' His shirt was, if anything, even dirtier than Jerry's.

'You could have washed them in the sink in your room,' said Wodger. His shirt was clean but wrinkled. He'd clearly forgotten to bring an iron with him.

'You should have asked me,' said June. 'I'd have done them for you.'

Oily coughed loudly. 'Maybe we ought to postpone the housekeeping debate,' he said. 'They seem to be waiting for us.'

He was right. Directly across the road which divided the front of The Maiden's Arms from the village green our opponents stood waiting for us.

On one side of them a blackboard had been erected and a small boy was standing ready with a stub of chalk and a damp cloth to write up the scores. Next to the blackboard an elderly, white haired gentleman sat in an aluminium framed garden chair. He had a large book spread out on his knees and was clearly the official scorer. Half a dozen spectators were gathered around the blackboard waiting for the match to begin. Across the other side of the green a man was taking his dog for a walk.

Wodger won the toss for the first time since the introduction of the current lbw laws. He seemed more surprised than anyone and quite uncertain about what to do.

'What would you like to do?' he asked the opposing captain.

'It's your choice!' Tony Parsons pointed out. 'You won the toss!'

'I don't want to appear impolite or pushy,' said Wodger timidly. 'It's your home ground after all . . .'

'No, really . . .' said Tony. 'You choose.'

Wodger looked around for help. 'What do you think?' he asked the rest of us. He had clearly never expected to win the toss and find himself faced with such a dilemma.

'Let's bat,' said Oily.

'Let's field,' said Jerry simultaneously.

We voted on it.

It must have been the first time in history that such a simple decision was taken in such a complicated, albeit democratic, way. By six votes to five we voted to field first.

Their innings was opened by two schoolboys who marched out to the wicket as though they couldn't wait to get started on our bowling. One was tall, slim and bespectacled. The other was also very slim but was much shorter. Both wore elbow protectors, chest protectors, thigh pads and helmets. Their shirts and flannels, bright white and neatly ironed, contrasted vividly with our own grass stained gear. For a moment I felt a twinge of embarrassment as I looked around and realised how scruffy we must look. Then I noticed the dandelions growing in the middle of the wicket and felt considerably better. Our shirts might not always be white but visitors have never found dandelions growing on our municipal pitches.

One of the youthful openers strutted down the wicket and knocked the heads off a couple of dandelions with his bat. He exchanged a word or two with his partner and they both laughed.

Kurt, our ecclesiastical opening bowler, who was waiting at his mark for the umpire to give him the signal to begin our bowling attack, was neither impressed nor amused by this light hearted display of quiet confidence. When, with the batsmen settled, the umpire finally lowered his arm and gave the vicar permission to bowl he glowered, lowered his head and charged up to the delivery crease like a bull who's been enraged by a particularly cocky young matador.

It was, I'm sure, a result of pure chance that the ball landed on one of the discarded dandelion heads and kicked sharply upwards and slightly to the right. The batsman, the taller of the two, the one whose attempt at gardening had left the dandelion head lying on the pitch, was preparing a neat forward defensive stroke that would have served him well had the ball followed a predictable route.

The ball missed the bat by an embarrassingly large distance, and hit the youthful opener just below his breastbone. Startled and winded the batsman was bent double by the blow. He dropped his bat and slowly fell backwards onto his stumps.

First ball. One wicket. No runs.

*　　*　　*

CHAPTER TWENTY ONE

Nothing inspires a fast bowler more than hitting a batsman and taking a wicket at the same time.

While the unfortunate youth limped slowly off the pitch the vicar, who seemed unaware of the role played by the decapitated dandelion head, explained exactly how he'd managed to dig the ball in and make it rise so unpredictably. Solemnly, we all congratulated him and shook his hand. June kissed him on the cheek.

Tony Parsons came in next and before he took strike he carefully removed the two dandelion heads from the wicket. He looked around, glowered at each of us in turn and after taking instructions from the umpire dug himself a small hole with the tip of his bat. When Oily, fielding at second slip, muttered something about gardening and planting dandelions Parsons turned round and awarded him a second glower.

The vicar thundered in to deliver his second ball of the match with all the fire and fury of a man who smells blood and wickets. I've noticed this about other clergymen; they always seem to have a robust attitude towards causing their opponents physical harm.

Parsons, however, was not about to be intimidated. And this time the vicar did not have any dandelion heads to help him.

Parsons played the same shot that his young predecessor had tried to play. This time it worked. Parsons' angled bat smothered the ball, taking nearly all the pace off it and allowing it to dribble out towards Wodger fielding at mid-on.

The rest of the over continued in much the same way. The vicar hurtled in as though determined to drill a hole clean through the opposing captain and the oppositions captain leant forwards and successfully used the blade of his bat to stun the ball and allow it to bounce harmlessly back down the pitch.

Jerry's first over from the other end was less successful and more expensive.

The shorter of the two schoolboy openers seemed distinctly unimpressed by Jerry's bowling and after hitting his first delivery fearlessly through the covers for a well run two, and glancing his second delivery past Arthur's outstretched gloves for a boundary, he stepped boldly down the wicket and hit Jerry's third ball straight back over his head.

The ball crossed the edge of the village green at a height of about twenty feet and crashed into the back of a passing builder's lorry.

Since it was the only decent match ball the home side owned we all sat down while a member of the batting side climbed into his car and chased after the lorry.

By the end of the fourth over we had lost our initial advantage. Our opponents had scored 34 runs for the loss of just one wicket.

Jerry and the vicar were, by now, both taking so much punishment that Wodger decided to 'rest' them early and bring on Simon and Brian instead.

Simon struck almost immediately. His third ball slipped between the remaining opener's bat and his pads and to the absolute astonishment of the home side Arthur performed a remarkable stumping. For a moment neither of the batsmen nor the umpire were quite prepared to believe what they'd seen. It wasn't by any means the first time I've seen cricketers wishing that they could watch an instant slow motion reply on a television screen.

But the evidence was incontrovertible. The batsman had missed the ball and Arthur hadn't. The wicket was shattered and the bails scattered and the batsman's rear foot was a good six inches outside his crease.

The next two batsmen didn't last long. Brian had one caught behind the wicket before he'd scored and the other was bowled by Simon and distracted by Sharon who was well aware of the effect her presence had on opposition batsmen and was determined to see that her newfound lover benefitted more than anyone else.

By now the home side had reached 50 but they had lost four wickets. The match seemed evenly poised.

The next batsman to join Tony Parsons at the crease looked to be by far the oldest member of their team. He was of average height and rather plumper than his team-mates. Almost bald he had two tufts of blond hair – one on each side of his head – and had, in that strange way favoured by vain and balding men, combed a dozen thin strands of hair across the dome of his head in a futile attempt to disguise his hairlessness.

As he walked out to the crease his eyes were closed and he talked incessantly to himself. He must have practised the walk a number of times for he was no more than a yard or two from the wicket when he finally opened his eyes.

Before even looking down the pitch at the umpire, to take his guard, he played a variety of practice air shots. Lots of batsmen play a few imaginary shots either on the way to the wicket or when they get there. I've done it myself a few times when I've felt my nerves jangling a bit. But this balding fellow didn't just play a couple of imaginary shots to help relax himself. He went through his whole repertoire of shots. And as he did so he talked constantly to himself; offering words of support and encouragement.

Eventually, after what seemed like a short lifetime, he abandoned his mental exercises and announced that he was ready to play. He took guard, exchanged a few cheery words with his captain, Tony Parsons, and settled down with Sharon's straining blouse (top four buttons undone) about a yard away from him and filling a large corner of his field of vision.

With the unfortunate fellow's imagination tuned to peak performance – and Sharon's cleavage providing more than ample inspiration – it is hardly surprising that he didn't seem to see the ball that Simon delivered to him. In fact he didn't even move. The ball, slow and slightly over-pitched – bounced once without deviating from its course and neatly flicked off a bail before landing safely in Arthur's gloves.

The hapless batsman remained motionless for a moment, frozen by mixed emotions. He looked at the umpire, turned and looked at the bail now lying on the grass and, after one long, last lingering look in Sharon's direction, started the slow walk back to the edge of the village green.

For the next long hour or so everything went the home side's way. Neither our bowlers nor our two busty fielders could stop the batsmen scoring almost at will. As he watched the home side's score mount to an almost impregnable level Wodger tried just about everything. He even let June and Sharon try a couple of overs.

Nothing worked. By four o'clock the home side had reached a total of 165 for the loss of just five wickets. When they declared, twenty minutes later, they had 201 runs on the board and Wodger was having difficulty in finding anyone prepared to bowl.

Jerry bowled the last over of our innings and after the fourth ball (which Parsons had dispatched to the boundary with disdain) the two home side batsmen met in the middle of the wicket and then, when they returned to their respective creases, proceeded to begin digging at the pitch with the ends of their bats.

'Hey!' cried Wodger. 'Be careful!'

'Just look at this!' said Parsons, digging at the pitch with the toe of his boot. 'Weeds!' He kicked a dandelion root out of the pitch and flicked it sideways with his boot. The removal of the dandelion root left a large hole in the ground.

'It's as bad down here!' said the batsman at the other end. He too had managed to kick a dandelion root out of the ground.

Wodger, Jerry, Oily, the vicar and I gathered around and stared at the wicket. Both holes had been dug on a good length.

'You can't do that!' complained the vicar. 'That's not cricket!'

'Sorry!' Parsons apologised. 'Only just noticed them.' He settled back into position, ready to receive the next ball. 'Can't have dandelions growing on the wicket.'

'I've half a mind to call the match off!' said Wodger, who was so indignant that he had gone bright red. 'It's disgwaceful!'

'Can't do that ...' said Oily, shaking his head sadly. 'It'll look as though we don't think we can match their score.'

'We can't!' Jerry pointed out.

'We might be able to.' The vicar insisted.

We carried on, of course. They scored six off the last two balls of the over and then declared.

In The Maiden's Arms the atmosphere was gloomy.

Simon, who said he was hungry, asked the barmaid if there were any sandwiches to go with the tea she'd served.

Our astonishment and despair reached new heights when she handed Simon a copy of the bar menu and told him that he could have another ploughman's lunch if he wanted one but that he'd have to pay for it.

'What?' said Oily. 'No sandwiches?'

'I'm afraid not,' said the barmaid, rather sniffily.

None of us had ever played a cricket match where the home side didn't provide sandwiches and cakes between innings. Hungry but glum we ordered more bread, cheese and apples. We realised, too late, why the home side had remained out on the village green when Tony Parsons had told us that we'd find refreshments available inside The Maiden's Arms.

Two minutes later one of the home side's young opening batsmen poked a head into the bar to tell us that the umpires were ready and to ask us, on behalf of Mr Parsons, if we'd like to start our innings. When he'd gone the barmaid asked us if we'd like the cost of our tea putting on our bill or if we'd rather pay cash.

*   *   *

CHAPTER TWENTY TWO

'I weally want to win this match,' said Wodger, buckling on his pads. He struggled for a moment with a troublesome buckle and then straightened up. 'Have you ever thought how similar a modern day cricketer is to a mediaeval knight preparing for the jousts?'

I thought for a moment and then shook my head.

'No.'

'Your trouble,' said Wodger dolefully, 'is that you've got no soul.' He pulled on his gloves, picked up his bat and tapped Jerry on the shoulder. 'Come on,' he said. 'Let's show them what we're made of.'

The rest of us watched as Wodger and Jerry tiptoed across the road, their spikes clattering against the tarmacadam, and then marched purposefully out towards the wicket. We watched as Wodger gave Jerry some last minute advice. We watched as Wodger took guard and then we watched as he received the first ball. Then we watched poor Wodger hobble back across the village green, across the road and up the pathway to the pub's front door.

'It pitched stwaight in that damned hole one of them dug!' complained Wodger, bitterly disappointed. He made a move as though intending to throw his bat down into a corner of the room, then thought better of it and placed it carefully on the floor.

'Never mind,' said Simon, 'Oily's probably bought up the umpires. We'll be all right, you'll see!' Sharon who was holding his left hand with her right leant across and kissed him on the cheek.

'Simon!' said Wodger sharply. 'That's not how this team

wins its matches!'

'Sorry!' said Simon. He blushed. 'Just a joke.'

'I should think so,' said Wodger, struggling to unbuckle his pads. The rest of us devoted our full attention to the cricket.

At first we thought that Wodger's dismissal might herald a painful and embarrassing defeat for us. But slowly Jerry and Oily managed to give us hope; not of victory, that seemed an impossible dream, but at least of a spirited and courageous defeat. As Norman put it, we wanted Mr Parsons and his team to know that they'd been involved in a cricket match!

Jerry was out at five minutes past five with his personal score on 23. We had lost two wickets and scored 47 runs.

'117!' said Wodger suddenly. He had been hunched over a notebook.

Puzzled, we looked at him.

'My total for the tour,' Wodger explained. He sighed and shook his head sadly. 'I weckon each wun has cost me about £3.50.'

Jerry stamped into the bar and threw down his bat. It bounced off the floor and collided with a small table, knocking an empty glass onto the floor. The glass bounced and rolled underneath one of the benches.

'Did you see that?' he demanded. 'The ball missed my bat by at least six inches! How that wicket keeper had the nerve to appeal for a catch I'll never know.' He sighed loudly and shook his head. 'As for the umpire ...' he began. He didn't finish but sat down noisily next to Wodger.

Slowly, as the light began to fade, we clawed our way towards the formidable total accumulated by the home team. Somewhere across the village the church bells began to ring. In the tops of a clump of trees which stood on one edge of the village green a dozen rooks gossiped and chattered.

As dusk fell the lights in homes around the green seemed much brighter than before and the lights of passing motor cars seemed to shine with enhanced brilliance.

The dusk helped neither side. The fielders found it more and more difficult to pick out the ball against the gloomy background of houses and trees and shadowy sky. On several occasions simple catches were missed. Twice in one over fielders allowed us to score boundaries when we should have

170

been restricted to singles. As batsmen we found that the poor light didn't just make it difficult for us to pick out the ball as it left the bowler's hand but also made it difficult for us to know exactly where the ball was when we were running between the wickets. Brian O'Toole was run out calling for a second run when the ball was already on its way back to the wicket keeper.

At around 8.00pm we slowly began to realise that we had a chance of winning. We had 150 runs on the blackboard and had lost 7 wickets.

When Oily was caught on the boundary after hitting a magnificent 85 I was joined at the wicket by Arthur, by far our most experienced player. When he arrived at the crease he called me down the wicket to join him for a moment.

'We can do this,' he said, swaying slightly from side to side as he spoke. 'Let's get em in boundaries and singles.'

I looked at him for a moment. Then he grinned broadly. I'd never heard Arthur attempt a joke before.

'Good idea!' I agreed.

Slowly, we edged closer and closer to the target. It got so dark that at one stage Tony Parsons approached us and suggested that we get some local motorists to line up their cars around the edge of their green so that we could play in their headlights.

'No, thanks!' said Arthur firmly.

'Why not?' I asked him puzzled.

'Three reasons,' he said. 'First, I can never see the damned ball anyway. I'm used to it. Second, if they're worried and we don't seem to be then we have an advantage.'

'And third?'

'Third,' said Arthur, 'if there are cars shining their headlights onto the field we'll be the ones to be blinded.'

'Why?' I asked. I honestly didn't understand.

'Think about it!' said Arthur, patiently. 'We'll be looking out towards the lights – the fielders will be looking in towards the wicket – with the lights behind them.'

And so we played on in the dark.

At ten minutes past nine, with the village green lit by the moon, I was still at the crease and Simon, our last man, had joined me. We needed just 5 runs to win.

I didn't even see where the last ball of our innings pitched, though my hearing was by now so acute that I could more or less tell where it was by listening to the sound it made. Realising that the ball was going to miss my off stump, and well aware that if I hit the ball hard I would probably get away with it even if I edged it to a fielder, I threw my bat at the ball with all the power I could find.

The ball caught the leading edge of my bat and shot away into the darkness. I didn't have the faintest idea where it had gone but called out to Simon to run. A few moments later, as we turned for the third run, we heard people shouting.

'What's happening?' asked Simon, as we passed in mid wicket.

'Heaven knows!' I said. 'Just keep running!'

It was only a minute or so later, when we had completed the winning run and were surrounded by the rest of the team, that Simon and I discovered that a small dog being taken for its evening walk had picked up the ball and run off with it.

'It wasn't fair!' complained Tony Parsons, in the bar an hour later. He wasn't a good loser.

'The ball was still in play,' said Wodger, 'and the umpires were happy about it.'

'They should have called a dead ball,' moaned Parsons for the umpteenth time.

'It wouldn't have made any diffewence,' said Wodger boldly. 'We were cwusing to victowy anyway.'

For the first time Parsons was speechless. He opened his mouth as though to say something but shut it again without breaking his silence.

*   *   *

We spent what was left of the evening telling one another stories in The Maiden's Arms. At eleven o'clock Oily and Simon went out and fetched us all a fish and chip supper which we ate sitting on the low wall outside the front of the pub.

'I'd like to propose a toast,' said Oily, putting down his chip wrapper and picking up his pint. 'To Wodger! Without whom none of this would have been possible!'

172

'To Wodger!' we cried in unison.

Wodger looked touched.

'Thank you!' he said. He got up off the stone wall and looked around at each of us in turn. June and the vicar were sitting arm in arm as were Simon and Sharon. The rest of us looked the same as ever, a little grubbier maybe, rather wearier than usual perhaps.

'Back to reality tomorrow,' said Norman glumly.

'Look at it this way,' said Oily, 'if we didn't spend the next 50 weeks coping with reality we wouldn't enjoy next year's tour half as much!'

'To next year's tour!' said Arthur, draining his whisky flask.

We all drank to that.

*　　*　　*